Camp Club Girls

Bailey's
PEORIA PROBLEM

Edited by Jeanette Littleton

ISBN 978-1-60260-272-4

Cover design © Thinkpen Design

Published by Barbour Publishing, Inc., P.O. Box 719, Uhrichsville, Ohio 44683, www.barbourbooks.com

Our mission is to publish and distribute inspirational products offering exceptional value and biblical encouragement to the masses.

 Member of the
Evangelical Christian
Publishers Association

Printed in the United States of America.

Dickinson Press, Inc.; Grand Rapids, MI; April 2010; D10002265

Camp Club Girls

Bailey's
PEORIA PROBLEM

Linda McQuinn Carlblom

BARBOUR
PUBLISHING

Almost Rammed!

"Look out!"

Alexis turned to see a huge ram lower his head and charge.

"Ahhhhhhh!" Alexis screamed. She sprinted through the herd of sheep toward the fence.

Baaa! Baaaaah! The sheep complained as they tripped out of her way.

Thud-thud-thud-thud! Alex could hear the angry ram close behind.

Chaotic baaing continued as more sheep were disrupted from their peaceful grazing.

Fwap! Alexis smacked into the fence. She frantically hopped up the first rung, swung her leg over the top rung, and fell to the ground below. Safe! She was out of the sheep pen in record time.

Pumph! The angry ram smacked his horns into the fence then darted off to the other side of the pasture.

"Are you okay?" Nine-year-old Bailey helped her friend stand up. As Alexis got up, she couldn't quite hide the fear in her eyes.

"I—I think so." Alex brushed off her jeans, and Bailey

noticed her friend's hands tremble. "Did I do something to make him mad?"

Bailey shook her head, her silky black hair swinging around her face. "Uncle Nathan said that one—Brutus—is just plain mean. Sometimes he even keeps Brutus in a different pen."

"Wish I'd known that before I went in there," Alex said.

Bailey put her arm around Alex. "I'm sorry. I should have been more careful about seeing which sheep were in there first. I know you're not used to being around farm animals."

"I'm hardly used to being around city animals! I've never even had a pet—unless you count my brothers."

Bailey laughed. "Well, I'll try to remember to check the pen next time."

"Who said anything about a next time?" Alex gave Bailey a playful nudge. "Anyway, it's not your fault. I should have kept my eyes open and noticed that ram."

"What's all the commotion over here?" Bailey's Uncle Nathan strode up behind them, the gravel crunching beneath his heavy work boots. Shy, his Australian shepherd, pranced at his side. Nathan's stocky, muscular build told of his hard work on Curly Q Ranch, which he had bought seven years earlier. His straight black hair was just long enough on top to ripple in the soft breeze.

"Brutus charged Alex," Bailey explained in a nutshell.

Uncle Nathan frowned as he looked at Alex. "Are you hurt?"

"No. I'm fine. Though I've never been so scared in all my twelve years."

"I'm sorry. I should have moved him to another pen before letting you girls come out here."

Bailey giggled. "You should have seen her move and jump over this fence! It was pretty funny now that I think about it."

Alex laughed, too. "Guess that cheerleading camp trained me pretty well! I never dreamed it would help me be limber enough to scale fences!"

"I'm just glad you're okay," Uncle Nathan said. "I put your suitcases in the upstairs room next to Brian's. Are you ready for the grand tour of Curly Q?"

Shy, a medium-sized white dog with black and gray splotches of color, sniffed Bailey's hand. Scratching her behind the ears, Bailey answered the uncle she adored. "You bet! But what about Brian? Is he coming?" She never grew tired of spending time with her older cousin, in spite of his friendly teasing and practical jokes.

"I don't think so. He got a call from a friend just as I walked out." Her uncle cupped one leathery hand around his mouth and muttered into Bailey's ear, "Probably some pretty girl. You know how teenagers are!" He winked. "Come on. I'll show you the pasture where most of the sheep are grazing today."

Bailey and Alex followed Uncle Nathan to a lush green field of clover. As they approached, the musky smell of sheep greeted them and the sheep's bleating grew increasingly louder.

"Here they are." Uncle Nathan leaned on the fence,

watching his herd as he had no doubt done every day for the past seven years.

"Wow." Alex's mouth gaped as she scanned the herd. "I've never seen so many sheep. How many are there?"

"Three hundred twenty-three," he answered confidently.

"Are you sure? How do you know one hasn't run off or something?"

Nathan chuckled. "A good shepherd knows his flock. He keeps count of them and watches their behavior. If one is missing, he knows it."

"Like Jesus," Bailey piped in. "He knows us and watches us, too. He's the Good Shepherd."

"Hey, yeah," Alex said. "I read that in my Bible, but it makes more sense now, seeing these poor helpless sheep. They really do need someone to take care of them, don't they—except for Brutus."

"Absolutely." Nathan rubbed the woolly head of a sheep that had wandered over to the fence. "They rely completely on their shepherd to care for them."

"Listen." Bailey cocked her head. "I love how they have different voices just like people. Some are low and others are higher."

"And they have different personalities like people do, too," Uncle Nathan added. "You really do get to know them after a while."

"Look at that baby!" Alex giggled as she pointed.

"Let's name her," Bailey suggested. "She's so cute. Look how she bounces around when she plays—like she has springs in her feet!" Bailey put her hands to the ground and sprang up and down imitating the lamb.

"How 'bout we call her Snowball?" Alex rubbed the lamb's woolly white head when it came close.

"Or Marshmallow," Bailey offered.

"I know!" Alex pulled the stretchy red hair bow from her ponytail, causing her dark brown curls to fall to her shoulders. She put the bright hair tie around the lamb's neck. "Let's call her Bow!"

"Bow it is." Bailey caressed the lamb's face. "You look beautiful, Bow!"

"Will you start shearing the sheep today?" Alex looked at Uncle Nathan.

He checked his watch. "We can probably get some done this afternoon before suppertime. I'll show you how, and then you can have a go at it."

"Do you do it right out there in the field?"

Nathan laughed. "Naw, we'll take them over to the barn. We shear on a nice clean floor so the wool doesn't get dirty when it falls. Also, the sheep getting sheared in the barn won't upset the others waiting their turn in the field."

"They don't like getting sheared?"

"It doesn't hurt them, but they don't like being held still. They can make an awful racket."

Alex grimaced. "I don't think sheep shearing will be my thing."

"I hope you'll try it. I think you'd do fine," Bailey assured her. "But you do have to be strong and determined to do it.

They need to know you're in charge."

"That's right." Uncle Nathan patted Alex on the back. "You city girls can do more than you think. You'll see. Now, why don't you and Bailey go change into your grubbies, grab us some bottles of water from the kitchen, and meet me in the barn. We're bound to get thirsty as we work. In the meantime, I'll bring out a couple of ewes and show you how it's done."

Bailey and Alex raced back to the house. The screen door slammed behind them, and they nearly collided with sixteen-year-old Brian in the kitchen.

"Hey! Slow down! I was just coming out to see you." Brian's bear hug lifted his younger cousin off her feet.

Bailey laughed as he returned her to the floor. "Brian, this is my friend, Alexis Howell. Alex for short."

"Nice to meet you." Brian extended his hand.

Alex smiled and pumped Brian's hand. Her cheeks turned rosy as she studied his handsome features—thick, wavy black hair that hung loosely around his face and ears, and a brilliant smile that showed off his ridiculously white teeth. His almond-shaped eyes danced almost as playfully as Bailey's. He had his dad's strong build and was already as tall as his father.

"We're after some water, and then Uncle Nathan is going to show Alex how to shear," Bailey told him.

"Looks like you're not wasting any time getting down to business. I'll go with you."

As Bailey turned to the refrigerator for the water

bottles, her eyes caught the *Peoria Daily News* on the kitchen table. Its primary front-page headline—MISSING MILLIONAIRE TO BE DECLARED LEGALLY DEAD?—aroused her curiosity, and she quickly scanned the article.

"Check this out," Bailey said to her friend.

"What?"

"This newspaper says an eccentric millionaire named Marshall Gonzalez has been missing for more than seven years. He lived around here. Distant relatives living in California want him to be declared legally dead so they can inherit his fortune. It says he has no near relatives and had few friends. Look. Here's his picture."

Alex came closer to inspect the photo. A plump Mexican man with a moustache and thick black eyebrows stared back at her. He wore a dark suit and tie. "I wonder where they live in California. Maybe it's close to Sacramento where I live." Alex wrapped a strand of curly dark hair around her finger.

"Maybe we can find out more from Uncle Nathan and Aunt Darcy at supper. We'd better change. I'm so glad your parents let you come to spend spring break with me!"

"Me, too!"

Minutes later, Bailey and Alex, dressed in worn jeans and old T-shirts, met Uncle Nathan in the barn. Alex pulled her hair back into a ponytail again at Bailey's advice. "It'll keep it out of your eyes while you work. I'd wear mine in a ponytail, too, if it was long enough." They spotted Brian in the pasture tending the sheep.

"Ready to get started?" Uncle Nathan asked.

Bailey looked at Alex and saw the color drain from her face. "I'm ready," she said, "but I think maybe Alex would rather watch this first time."

"You got that right. I'm not excited about getting too close to those animals after that last encounter."

"No problem. We'll take it slow, and you can just watch for now." Uncle Nathan patted the two ewes with thick, curly fleece that stood near him. Thin legs poked out the bottom of their fleece, reminding Bailey of cartoon sheep. Though she'd seen sheep many times over the years, she still giggled at how funny they looked.

"Nowadays most ranchers use electric shears like this." Uncle Nathan held up the shears so Alex could see. They hung from the end of a long cable leading to an electric motor attached to the barn ceiling. In a flash, he lifted the struggling sheep's chin and brought the animal to a sitting position on its rump, while holding the ewe between his strong legs. In this position, the ewe's struggling ceased, and Uncle Nathan began shearing. He ran long strokes down the length of the sheep's body before flipping it over and doing the other side. Uncle Nathan then sheared the sheep's belly and legs. In a matter of minutes, the once fat, roundish animal looked years younger and not so wise.

"That's amazing!" Alex said. "How'd you do that so fast?"

"Years of practice," Uncle Nathan answered. "But speed isn't the important thing. If you rush, you might accidentally nick the sheep, and the next time you try to shear them, you'll have a mighty fight on your hands. My sheep trust me. They know I'm careful with them. But I try to get it done as quickly and carefully as possible so they don't have to be held still too long."

"Can I try it now? I'll probably be a bit rusty." Bailey looked at her uncle expectantly.

"After we sweep up this wool. Remember, we have to separate the belly wool from the rest of the fleece so we can bag it separately. Then we need to skirt, bag, and label all of it."

"Skirt? What's that?" asked Alex.

"It's how we roll the fleece to get it ready for market," Bailey answered, proud that she knew the answer.

Uncle Nathan showed Alex how to skirt the fleece, and together they placed it in a plastic garbage bag. "We get more money at market if we have the different wools separated and labeled properly," he explained.

"Now?" Bailey asked, bobbing up and down on her toes. Her hand held the shears.

"Sure thing. I'll be right here in case you need my help."

Bailey flipped on the shears and used her legs to hold the old ewe. She ran the tool deftly across the sheep's skin, the wool dropping on the cleanly swept, concrete barn floor.

Alex stepped forward to watch more closely. It took Bailey twice as long as it had Uncle Nathan, but she got the job done.

"There!" Bailey smiled with satisfaction as she wiped sweat from her forehead.

"You were magnificent!" Alex exclaimed. "I can't believe

you could handle the sheep like that!"

"You want to try?" Bailey asked her friend.

Alex hesitated. "I think I'll watch awhile longer. I'm not sure I'm ready yet."

"Good call," Uncle Nathan said. "You can learn a lot from watching. Maybe you'll want to try it yourself in a day or two."

The wheels of a car crunched on the gravel driveway, drawing their attention.

"Aunt Darcy!" Bailey took off running, black hair flying.

Aunt Darcy scrambled out of the car and caught her niece in a giant hug. "It's so good to see you! Let me see how tall you are."

Bailey stood stick straight as her aunt, still dressed in her nurse's uniform, used her hand to measure from the top of Bailey's head to herself. "You're up to my chin! You must have grown three inches since I saw you last!" Darcy spotted Alex standing a polite distance away. "This must be Alex. Welcome to the Curly Q! I'm so glad you could come with Bailey this year."

"Thanks for having me," Alex said as she edged closer. "I'm already learning so much!"

Alex stuck out her hand, and Aunt Darcy took it and pulled her into a hug. "I have plenty of those to go around," she said midhug. "I picked up some fried chicken, corn, and mashed potatoes on my way home from work. Anybody hungry?"

"Always!" Brian ambled in from the pasture and

overheard the question. "Let's eat!"

"Go wash up, all of you," Darcy instructed. "Looks like you could use it!"

"Race you to the house," Brian challenged.

Bailey and Alex were off like lightning, but Brian's long legs soon overtook them.

After everyone had washed up and changed into clean clothes, they sat around the table and joined hands. Uncle Nathan offered thanks to the Lord for the food and passed the bucket of chicken.

"Did you see the headline in the newspaper today about the missing millionaire?" Bailey ventured.

"Yes. That case has been in the news off and on for years." Uncle Nathan buttered a roll.

"Do you think he's really dead?" asked Alex.

"Hard to say. No one's seen or heard from him for seven years," Aunt Darcy said.

"That doesn't mean he's dead," Bailey countered.

"No, but it sure leaves a lot of unanswered questions," said Brian around a mouthful of food.

"What do you know about him, Uncle Nathan?" Bailey bit into her chicken leg.

"Not much. He kept to himself, just like the paper said. He didn't have any friends to speak of. Never married, no children."

"So you knew him?" Alex asked.

"No. Just that his name was Marshall Gonzalez," Uncle Nathan said. "I bought this ranch the year he disappeared.

et him, but I've heard talk of him. People thought
bit strange 'cause he was such a loner, but you
know how folks like to make up stories about others who
are different. Pass the corn, please."

Bailey passed the bowl and asked, "Do you know where
he lived?"

"Why all this interest in Mr. Gonzalez?"

"Just curious." Bailey glanced at Alex, who was trying to
tame a smile.

●—●—●

Bailey and Alexis headed up to their room at nine o'clock
that night.

"This used to be my cousin Jennifer's room," Bailey told
Alex. "But she moved out when she went to college last year."

"Which bed do you want?" Alex asked.

Twin beds flanked either side of a window that was
much taller than it was wide. Matching rose-covered
bedspreads adorned the beds, and a nightstand sat beside
each one. A soft pink beanbag chair slouched against the
wall parallel to the beds and window. Two walls were
papered pastel pink with tiny white dots. It reminded
Bailey of the dotted swiss material her mother would try
to talk her into for making her Easter dresses. It was fine
for wallpaper, but Bailey wouldn't want to wear it—or any
dress for that matter.

"I usually sleep in that one." Bailey pointed to the bed
closest to the adjoining bathroom.

"Okay." Alexis plopped her suitcase on the other bed
and started unpacking.

"I don't know about you, but something about this Marshall Gonzalez case seems weird." Bailey moved clothes from her suitcase to the top two dresser drawers, leaving the bottom two for Alex. "Why would distant relatives care about this guy now after seven years? Did they just find out about his disappearance?"

"I know what you mean," Alex agreed. "Maybe he's still alive." She dug in her suitcase for her toothbrush. "I'm going to take a quick shower."

"Okay. I'll take one when you're done. But let's think some more about this case."

• — • — •

After her shower, Bailey slipped into her silky pink capri pajamas with soft gray kitties on the pants.

Alex, already in her nightgown, grabbed her toothbrush and toothpaste and entered the steamy bathroom, leaving the door open. "Now about this Gonzalez case. We could make a list of what we know so far and what we still need to find out." Alex started brushing her teeth.

"Good idea. We'll need to work quickly on this since we only have a week until we have to go home." Bailey parked her empty rolling suitcase in the corner. She pulled back the sheets on her twin bed and put her traveling companion, a sandy brown stuffed dog named Ginger, on her pillow.

Alex spit out her toothpaste. "How will we be able to get away to investigate with all the sheep to shear?"

Bailey took a notebook from her backpack.

"Tomorrow's Sunday, silly. Uncle Nathan doesn't believe in working on the Sabbath. We'll go to church in the morning and just relax in the afternoon. Even on the other days we'll probably only shear in the morning. He knows kids need time to play. Usually after lunch we're free to do whatever we want. And believe me, after that long, you'll feel like you've worked all day!" Bailey began scribbling in the notebook.

"What do we have so far?" Alex asked, knowing Bailey was writing down clues.

"Not much, really. Just Marshall's name, and that he's a millionaire with distant relatives in California who want to declare him legally dead so they can inherit his money. He has no close relatives and very few friends. He's been missing for over seven years."

"It may not be much, but it's a start." Alex wiped her face with a cleansing pad, the antiseptic smell filling the room. "Obviously, the motive for wanting him to be declared dead is money."

"Right." Bailey took her turn in the bathroom now, toothbrush in hand.

"For starters, we should find out where Gonzalez lived, don't you think?"

Bailey nodded, her mouth foaming white. She spit and wiped her mouth on a towel. "I wonder how he got so rich."

"Good question. We'll check that out, too." Alex yawned.

"I think I'm gonna sleep good tonight. It's been a busy day." Bailey crawled into bed.

"Me, too, but I can't wait for tomorrow. We've got more than sheep shearing to do while we're here this week."

"Yeah! We've got a mystery to solve!"

The Mystery Man and the Mystery House

Sunday morning dawned bright but cool, as Bailey and Alex dressed for church.

"Maybe we can find out more about Marshall Gonzalez today," Bailey said, hairbrush in hand. She grimaced with the pull of every tangle in her fine hair.

"Probably won't be until later if we do. I doubt the sermon will be about Marshall," Alex joked.

After church, Bailey and Alex chowed down on burgers at the local Steak 'n Shake with Uncle Nathan, Aunt Darcy, and George and Helen Jones, a couple from their church. Brian took off to eat with his friends from the youth group.

"What do you make of the headlines these days?" asked Mr. Jones.

Uncle Nathan stuffed a plump fry into his mouth. "Which ones?"

"This business about Marshall Gonzalez." Mr. Jones sipped his soda. "You think he's really dead?"

Bailey and Alex shot excited glances at each other but kept eating while they listened.

"Hard to know for sure," Uncle Nathan said. "But

nobody's seen anything of him for a lot of years, so I guess he could be dead."

"Never found a body though," Mr. Jones added.

"This is hardly mealtime conversation, George." Mrs. Jones reached for the salt.

"Just talking about the news, dear," Mr. Jones said, patting his wife's hand.

"I heard Marshall lived not too far from here," Aunt Darcy added.

"That's a fact. Somewhere east of here is what I heard, though I don't know exactly where." Mr. Jones dipped his french fry in ketchup before popping it into his sizable mouth.

"I suppose if we'd bought the Curly Q a year earlier, we probably would've met him." Uncle Nathan sipped his soda.

"Very likely," Mr. Jones said. "We only moved here five years ago, so we didn't know him either. But they say he kept to himself, which is part of the problem of them not knowing what happened to him."

"Good heavens." Mrs. Jones pressed her napkin to her mouth.

Bailey nudged Alex and suppressed a giggle.

Alex nudged her back and disguised her smile with a cough.

"Are you okay, dear?" asked Mrs. Jones.

Alex took a giant gulp of water. "Yes, I'm fine."

"Well," Uncle Nathan continued, "you'd think someone would have befriended him."

"Maybe," Mr. Jones answered. "But a person can be pretty scarce if he wants to be."

"Was he really a millionaire?" asked Bailey.

"That's what they say." Uncle Nathan bit into his burger, juice dripping from its sides. He quickly grabbed a napkin to mop up the mess.

"How'd he get so rich?" Alex wondered aloud.

"He inherited his money," Mr. Jones responded. "From what I've heard, he didn't have the personality to be much of a businessman. He basically just let his fortune earn interest at the bank and spent his time doing whatever he pleased."

"Inherited his money," Bailey said under her breath. "Just like his relatives are hoping to do." She bit her bottom lip as she thought that over.

"About all anyone knows for sure is that he pretty much closed his house in Peoria and released all the people who worked for him, except for a caretaker." Uncle Nathan took a drink of his pop. "Some say he mentioned something about trying sheep herding before he took off, and had even attended a sheep expo at the state fair in Springfield."

"Then he must have had a sheep farm somewhere." Alex looked at Bailey.

"Only if he acted on what he was thinking about," Bailey said.

"So if he was hardly ever seen, even by his neighbors, how does anyone know when he disappeared?" asked Alex.

"Hmm." Uncle Nathan rubbed his chin. "That's a good question."

"Maybe he had secret business associates who reported him missing when they didn't hear from him," suggested Bailey.

"Or maybe his bank noticed he wasn't using any of his money," added Alex.

Mr. Jones raised his eyebrows and looked at Bailey and Alex. "You guys are good!"

"I've read a lot of Nancy Drew mysteries," Alex explained.

"And I'm just a natural detective." Bailey took a long draw on her straw, trying to get a taste of her thick chocolate milkshake.

"Naturally nosy is more like it," Uncle Nathan teased.

"Nathan!" Aunt Darcy scolded her husband.

Uncle Nathan mussed Bailey's hair playfully. "Aw, she knows I love her."

Bailey's black eyes sparkled at her uncle as she beamed and nodded.

The waitress soon brought the checks. Nathan and Mr. Jones stood and shook hands good-bye while the women exchanged hugs.

"Nice meeting you little ladies," Mr. Jones said to Bailey and Alex.

"Nice meeting you, too," Bailey answered.

"Let us know when you crack the Gonzalez case," Mr. Jones added, smiling broadly. "That'd show those authorities, wouldn't it? To have two girls figure it out when they've been working on it for years!" He laughed and smacked Uncle Nathan on the back.

●—●—●

Back at the Curly Q, Bailey and Alex changed out of their church clothes.

"What do you want to do?" Alex asked.

"It's a beautiful day now that the sun has warmed things up." Bailey's eyes twinkled. "I think we should take a walk."

"Ooh, good idea!"

"We probably won't even need our sweatshirts now, it's so nice out."

"Let's go!" Alex started for the bedroom door.

"Whoa, girl!" Bailey slowed her friend with an outstretched arm. "We need to gather some supplies first."

"Supplies? What for?"

"In case we happen to stumble on some clues for the Gonzalez case. I'll bring my notepad and my camera watch." Bailey rifled through her backpack.

"You have a camera watch?" Alex's eyes grew to the size of a CD.

"Yeah." Bailey nodded like a bobblehead. "Kate told me about them at camp last summer, so I checked them out online and added it to my birthday list. I got it from my dad when I turned nine in January but haven't had much chance to try it out yet."

"You're awesome!" Alex hugged Bailey. "Speaking of Kate, we really should call the other Camp Club Girls to let them in on our latest mystery."

"They may have ideas we haven't even thought of

yet," Bailey agreed. "I'll call Kate and Sydney, and you call Elizabeth and McKenzie. With all of us working together, we'll have this mystery solved by the end of the week!"

The girls sat on their beds and flipped open their cell phones.

"I'm so glad my parents finally got me a new cell phone before we came to Uncle Nathan's." Bailey bit her lip as she found Kate's number and pushed TALK. "Kate? It's Bailey!"

Alex, sitting cross-legged on her bed, chatted away to Elizabeth while Bailey filled Kate in on the details they already knew from the Gonzalez case. Then each one called the next girl they were assigned. A half hour later, Bailey and Alex had hung up.

"Did Kate have any ideas about this case?" Alex pushed her phone back into her jeans pocket.

"She's going to check the Internet for all the newspaper articles and public records she can find on Gonzalez," Bailey said. "And she's going to see if she can find an older online map of the area that might show exactly where his ranch was."

Alex did a cartwheel between the two beds, her cheerleading skills bursting to the surface. "Good work! That Kate is a genius!"

"How 'bout you? Did Elizabeth or McKenzie have any ideas?"

"Elizabeth will give it some thought and, of course, prayer. In the meantime, she said for us to be careful and not to get in over our heads."

Bailey laughed, knowing Elizabeth's tendency to worry, then added, "I know she really will take the praying part seriously. That's bound to help us!"

"Yeah," agreed Alex. "And McKenzie asked why Gonzalez was such a loner. She wondered if he had bad relations with his family or maybe never even knew his distant relatives. As she put it, there must be some reason he was so withdrawn."

"Hmm." Bailey's eyebrows wrinkled in thought. "I never thought of that. But she's right. It's not natural to avoid all other human contact. There must be more to his story."

"What about Sydney? Did she say anything?" Alex asked.

"Not much. She'll have to think it over. She said to call her as we get more to go on."

Alex nodded. "I told Elizabeth and McKenzie that we'd keep our phones charged, on, and with us at all times in case they need to contact us."

"Good." Bailey laughed. "Oh, and I forgot to tell you—Biscuit says hi!"

Alex burst out laughing. Biscuit was the dog they all found last summer at camp, but with Kate's parents' consent, it became Kate's dog after camp, since the two of them had grown especially close. Biscuit had even helped the Camp Club Girls solve their first mystery and had become known as the Wonder Dog.

"Good ol' Biscuit," Alex said, grinning broadly.

"I think we're ready for our walk now." Bailey patted her pockets. "I've got everything we need—notepad, pen, cell phone, and camera watch."

"Let's go, then!"

At the bottom of the stairs, Bailey called into the living room, "We're going for a walk! We'll be back in a little while!"

"Okay," Aunt Darcy answered.

"We have our cell phones," Alex offered.

"Good thinking. See you later."

The girls walked down the country road past huge oak trees that provided a cool canopy of shade. Small splashes of sunshine shone between the leaves. The sheep pasture was soon on their right, and the girls could hardly talk over the loud bleating. Alex covered her nose and mouth with her hand to block out the smell.

"Hey, look over there!" Bailey pointed beyond the pasture.

"What is it?" Alex squinted her eyes to see.

"I'm not sure yet. We'll have to get closer."

Alex and Bailey were almost jogging as they moved nearer to a run-down house.

"Boy, does that need a fresh coat of paint!" Bailey said. She was glad the noisy sheep would keep her voice from being heard by anyone but Alex.

"It's so far back from the road, it's still hard to tell, but it sure does look like it needs work," Alex agreed.

"Do you think anyone lives there?" Bailey asked.

Alex shook her head. "Who could live in a place like that?"

Both girls returned their gazes to the dilapidated house.

Moving closer, but still a safe distance away, they studied the place. Shutters hung crookedly from the front windows. A huge oak tree reached over the side of the house, scraping the sagging roof with every gust of wind. Some of the shingles were missing, and those still attached curled up like the front end of a toboggan. A porch wrapped around two sides of the house, but several posts were missing from the railing.

"Wow," Bailey finally said.

"Look at those weeds in the yard," Alex added. "I bet they're as tall as you are!"

"It looks haunted." Bailey pointed her watch toward the house and snapped a few pictures. "But it does make an interesting photo subject." They moved, and she took some from another angle.

"Aaaaack!" Brian jumped out from behind a tree.

The girls screamed and grabbed each other.

Brian doubled with laughter until he was red in the face. "You. . .should have. . .seen your faces!" he gasped then laughed some more.

"That was *not* funny!" Bailey's hands were in fists on her hips.

"It sure was from this angle." Brian wiped his eyes. "What are you guys doing anyway?"

"None of your business," Alex answered, eyes shooting daggers at him.

"We're just exploring, that's all," Bailey sputtered.

"Sounds fascinating." Brian rolled his eyes and turned

toward home. "See ya later. Sorry if I freaked you out. Feel free to send me your therapy bill." He laughed again as he turned toward home.

Bailey looked at Alex, her heart still pounding. "You okay?"

"Yeah." Alex tucked her curly hair behind her ears. "Guess we probably did look kind of funny." A smile overtook her fair-skinned face.

Bailey sighed. "I was afraid that would make you hate Brian."

"No. He really is pretty fun." Alex inhaled deeply to calm her nerves and then looked back to the old house. "All right. Now that we can breathe again, what next?"

"Maybe we should head back home."

"We could check our e-mail to see if the Camp Club Girls have sent us any updates," Alex suggested.

"Good idea." Bailey snapped one more picture.

"It'll be fun to see if the other girls turn up anything else."

Just then a muscular brown dog shot toward them from the house, teeth bared, barking and growling.

"Run!"

Bailey and Alex sprinted to the road. Bailey glanced over her shoulder and saw that the dog had stopped at the spot where they'd been taking pictures, though he continued to bark. She shivered at the thought of those teeth tearing through flesh and bone. The girls jogged the rest of the way home, Bailey wheezing with each breath.

When they reached their room, Bailey grabbed her

inhaler. She breathed in as she squeezed the puff of medicine into her mouth and held her breath for ten seconds as it took effect.

"You okay?" Alex asked.

Bailey nodded, still holding her breath.

"That asthma must be such a pain."

Bailey exhaled loudly. "It's not that bad. You just have to learn to manage it, like having your inhaler handy all the time. I should have taken it with me. But it's no big deal."

"Good." Alex gave Bailey one more worried look. "Then let's check our e-mail." She pulled out her laptop and booted it up.

"Right. And we could download these pictures, too." Bailey took off her watch. She pressed a button, and a tiny memory stick popped out. "I'll just slide this into the computer and. . ."

Photos popped up on Alex's laptop before Bailey even finished her sentence.

"Guess I need to get better at using this thing," Bailey said, glancing at her camera watch. The pictures, some blurry, others clear, passed by in a slide show on the computer screen.

"Wait a minute!" Alex whisper-yelled. "Go back to that last one!"

Bailey went back to a somewhat blurry picture of the front of the house. "What?" she asked.

"Look closely at that window on the left side."

Bailey looked at the picture then at Alex. "What?"

"I know it's not clear, but it almost looks like there's someone in the window."

Bailey peered closer at the fuzzy picture. "Maybe. . ."

"The person isn't right up close to the window, but it looks like someone may be inside that house," Alex insisted.

"Could be, but it's too hard to tell from this shot. Let's keep looking and then go back and take another look at all of them."

Alex nodded.

Though none of the photos were crystal clear, after reviewing them again, some did seem to show a shadowy image in the house.

"I still can't imagine that anyone would live in that place. It's such a mess!" Alex examined the picture more closely.

"Who knows? This image in the window may not even be a human." Bailey's voice dripped with disappointment. "It may just be a reflection of light or something."

"Or then again, it might not be!" Alex encouraged. "We just have to keep trying to get better pictures. It was your first try with your new gadget. You'll get better at it."

Bailey gave a tiny smile. "Do you think the other girls would be interested in seeing these just for fun?"

"The ones of the front of the house will at least give them a good idea of what it looks like. Even if the house doesn't have anything to do with our case, it's still interesting."

"Okay. I'll send them off." Bailey attached the best

photos to an e-mail and hit SEND. "They'll see what they're missing by not being here with us!"

"We may have two mysteries on our hands. One about Gonzalez and one about the haunted house!" Alex laughed.

"Yeah, but we definitely have to go back and get better shots." Bailey crossed her arms and frowned.

"Do we have time to go now before supper?" Alex asked.

Bailey looked at the clock on the wall. "Maybe if we hurry. It's almost five o'clock."

"Let's go!" Alex jumped up from the bed.

"Wait!" Bailey put her camera watch back on and dug for something in her backpack.

"What are you doing?"

"We need to take something to keep that dog away." Victoriously, Bailey held up a snack pack of cookies and then stuffed them in her pocket.

"Good thinking!"

They hurried down the stairs and through the kitchen.

"We're going back outside for a while," Bailey called as they passed Aunt Darcy.

Her aunt laughed. "I'll call you when it's suppertime."

The girls ran down the road back toward the old house. Suddenly Alex put her arm out in front of Bailey like a barricade and stopped abruptly. "Look!"

From about a quarter of a mile away, something—or someone—moved through the tall weeds in the front yard.

CHAPTER 3

Dude, Rude, and Yeller

"Did you see that?" Alex asked, struggling to keep her voice from trembling.

"I saw it, but I don't know what it was." Bailey squinted her eyes.

"It was either that mean dog jumping or someone standing and then crouching so we wouldn't see him."

"Are you sure?" Bailey's voice quivered.

"Not entirely, but that's what it looked like to me. One second it was tall, and the next it was gone."

"We need to find a place where we can watch but not be seen." Bailey looked around. "I've got it!"

Alex's full attention was on her younger friend.

"Uncle Nathan's sheep pasture backs right up to the run-down house's empty field. And that field is right next to the yard with the tall weeds. If we pretend we're tending the sheep in the pasture, we should be able to keep a watch on the yard without being too obvious."

"I don't know," Alex said. "We may be too far away to see much from there."

"Their field isn't very big, and if we stay toward the back

of the pasture, I think we'll have a pretty good view." Bailey pointed her index finger in the air dramatically. "*And* it will be safe. A creek separates our pasture from the empty field, as well as a fence."

"A creek? I never saw that!"

"It runs through a big culvert under the road, so you may not have seen it." Bailey grinned mischievously. "Besides the fact that we were running pretty fast on our way back!"

"You can say that again! I bet I could have beat Sydney in that race with the growling dog chasing us!" Alex laughed, thinking about their athletic friend who competed in the Junior Olympics in track and field.

"Well, shall we try watching from the pasture?" Bailey asked.

"Guess we could see what the view is like from there." Alex picked at a hangnail on her left thumb. "Uh, Bailey?"

"Yeah?"

"I haven't spent much time around sheep. Anything I should know?"

Bailey smiled reassuringly. "Just watch where you step."

Alex burst out laughing. "Thanks for the tip."

"Seriously, sheep are gentle. Why else would the Bible talk about them so much?"

"I guess. . ."

"Think about it." Bailey took hold of Alex's hand and swung it. "Jesus told his disciples He was sending them out like sheep among wolves. It's a comparison—a gentle

34

animal compared to a wild animal."

"I never thought of it like that."

The two walked back to the pasture and entered through the gate, being careful to close it behind them. They made their way through the flock of sheep, the smell almost knocking them over. Their favorite lamb, Bow, sprang over to them in excited leaps. The red bow Alex had put around her neck was still there, though not quite as bright and pretty as it had been. They bent down to pet the baby sheep, but the smell was too much.

"Can't we wear masks or something while we're in here?" Alex gagged, her hand over her mouth and nose.

"After you're around the smell awhile you don't notice it as much. But I think Uncle Nathan has some masks in the barn. We'll have to look for them next time we're in there."

As they neared the far end of the pasture, Bailey heard a faint cry. "Did you hear that?"

"I only hear sheep bleating."

They walked several steps further, and the sound came again, only louder.

"That's no sheep! Look!" Bailey pointed toward the haunted house.

Alex turned in the same direction and saw a man waving wildly to get their attention.

"Hey!" The man yelled, his arms high above his head.

Bailey looked at Alex, unsure what to do.

"I think he needs help!" Bailey said.

"We have to be careful," Alex reminded her. "We don't know that guy."

Bailey inched toward the man with Alex following close behind.

"We'll have to climb over the fence when we get to it," Bailey said.

The girls heard another yell and saw two more men appear in the distance, one wearing a cowboy hat. Bailey and Alex ducked behind two smelly sheep, peeking out just enough to see.

The two men grabbed the first man roughly and shoved him back toward the house. The first man's yelling stopped, but now the other two men hollered at him, though Bailey couldn't make out what they said. She saw the first man look over his shoulder in their direction one last time before being pushed through the front door.

Alex let out a breath she didn't know she'd been holding. "Guess we now know for sure someone is living there."

"As if Fang the dog wasn't enough to tell us that!" Bailey stood up slowly.

"Come on. We'd better go back home." Alex took Bailey's arm and turned to leave. "It's probably almost suppertime."

"We can't go now!" Bailey jerked away. "That guy needs our help!"

"Bailey, we can't go charging over there." Alex stood planted, hands on her hips. "You saw how rough those guys were. It's not safe!"

"Well, we have to do something! What if he's in danger?"

"Maybe we should tell your aunt and uncle," Alex suggested.

"I don't know." Bailey shook her head. "They might try to make us give up our sleuthing on the Gonzalez case."

"Look," Alex said, resting her hand on Bailey's shoulder. "How about if we pray about this and trust that God will show us the right thing to do?"

Bailey nodded. "I just hope He doesn't make us wait too long to show us."

Alex laughed. "I know. But remember, God loves that man just as much as He loves us. He'll protect him until we can figure out what to do."

"I guess you're right."

Bailey and Alex moved between the sheep, making their way back to the gate. Once out of the pasture, Bailey asked, "Why do you think those two men were so mean to the other guy?"

"Maybe he's supposed to be working for them and they thought he was out there goofing off," Alex suggested.

"Maybe." Bailey scratched her head. "Or maybe he was trying to get help for someone who's hurt inside the house and the other two guys don't want people to know about it. Maybe they're the ones who hurt him!"

Alex laughed. "You have a good imagination."

"Or what if they've kidnapped someone and are hiding him there, and the guy yelling was trying to help him!"

"Wow! You really should write books or something."

This time Bailey laughed. "I'd rather act. I love drama."

Alex's eyes flew open wide. "I didn't know that!"

"I've been in a school play, and I'd love to be in community theater."

"Why don't you?"

Bailey shrugged. "Just haven't gotten around to it yet. I'm only nine!"

Alex squeezed Bailey around the shoulders. "Someday you'll be a star."

"Not if I stay in Peoria, Illinois." Bailey's eyebrows wrinkled. "I need to get out of this town and go to Los Angeles or New York or somewhere big to do that. That's my plan anyway."

"Sounds like a good plan, but you can at least get started in Peoria."

"I guess." Bailey sighed and then smiled. "In the meantime, we need to figure out this Gonzalez mystery."

The girls reached their yard and smelled supper cooking.

"Mmm." Bailey put her nose in the air and sniffed. "Smells like spaghetti!"

"Yeah," Alex agreed as she opened the screen door, "and garlic bread!"

"Right on both counts." Aunt Darcy pulled the garlic bread out of the oven. "You're just in time to wash up and eat."

"Perfect timing," Bailey said as she and Alex headed to the bathroom to wash their hands.

After supper, Bailey and Alex went to their bedroom to check their e-mail.

Alex flopped stomach-down onto her bed, opened the laptop in front of her, and waited for it to boot.

"I hope one of the other girls has already sent us some

information on Gonzo." Bailey hopped onto the bed beside Alex to see.

"Gonzo?" Alex questioned.

"Yeah. Marshall Gonzalez," Bailey explained.

Alex laughed and gave Bailey a playful shove. "I should have known it was only a matter of time until you gave him a nickname."

"I was thinking those guys we saw today should have names, too." Bailey closed her eyes for a moment. "How about Yeller for the first guy 'cause he yells so much, and Dude and Rude for the other two, since the one wore a hat like an old cowboy dude and they both treated Yeller rudely?"

Alex rolled to her back and laughed. "Dude and Rude it is," she said. "And Yeller!"

"Hey look! We got something from Kate!" Bailey pointed at the computer screen.

"And it has an attachment." Alex opened the e-mail, and Kate's short note appeared:

Still checking on the Gonzalez stuff. He was good at staying out of the public eye. Will let you know when I find anything. In the meantime, here's a picture of Biscuit doing his latest trick—dancing with me on his hind legs.

Alex clicked on the YouTube link, and a healthy and happy Biscuit appeared standing on his back legs, front paws in Kate's hands. The girls laughed at the photo.

"He should be on *Pet Stars*!" Alex pirouetted around the room like a ballerina.

"Wow! Look how big he got!" Bailey leaned in to get a closer look at the small light brown and white mutt with fur hanging over his big brown eyes. "He's twice the size he was at camp last summer."

"Yeah, but he still only comes to Kate's waist when he's stretched out dancing." Alex's eyes softened. "Aww. He's so cute!"

"And so clean!" Bailey added. "Remember how dirty and matted he was when we found him?" The two girls sat quietly for a moment.

"But no news on Gonzo yet," Bailey said, getting back to business.

"Well at least she's working on it." Alex closed her laptop.

"Oh man!" Bailey slapped her leg in disgust.

"What?"

"I should have taken pictures of Yeller, Dude, and Rude with my camera watch!"

"O–o–h yeah." Alex snapped her fingers. "But you couldn't have done that without being seen. It's probably best you didn't."

"But then we'd have pictures to examine and to send to the other Camp Club Girls. Maybe Kate could even match it with someone on the Internet."

"That would have been helpful, for sure."

"Maybe we'll see them again sometime."

"Even if we do, safety comes first." Alex looked firmly at Bailey. "No pictures if it will put us in danger."

Bailey stared her down.

"Deal?" Alex pushed.

Bailey dropped her gaze and sighed. "Deal," she said.

"Now, what's our schedule for tomorrow?" Alex asked, trying to lighten the mood.

"Well, tomorrow's Monday, so I guess we'll start early with sheep shearing." Bailey perked up at that thought.

"I guess it will be time for me to give it a try, huh?" Alex started picking her nails.

"Uncle Nathan and I can each do one while you watch. Then you can have a turn. You'll do great."

"I'm kind of excited and kind of nervous all at the same time."

Bailey's eyes sparkled with mischief. "If you don't mind me saying, you're looking a bit sheepish."

Alex groaned. "That was a *ba–a–a*–d joke!"

"You even sound like a sheep! Sorry, I couldn't resist." Bailey tucked her hair behind her ear. "Really, don't worry. I felt nervous, too, when I was learning. But you'll see it's not that hard."

"I hope so."

"And remember you don't have to do it fast like Uncle Nathan. He just does it that way 'cause he's had so much practice."

"I know. I'll take my time."

"I read once that a professional can shear a sheep in less than two minutes," Bailey said.

Alex's jaw dropped. "Two minutes! That's fast!"

"And not only that, he removes the fleece all in one piece!" Bailey held up one finger.

"You've got to be kidding. How is that possible?"

"I don't know, but that's what the magazine said."

Alex giggled. "Something tells me I won't master that this week."

"Me neither!" Bailey rolled her eyes dramatically.

"We need to update the other Camp Club Girls on those men we saw," Alex said.

"This time I'll call Elizabeth and Sydney," Bailey said as she flipped open her phone, "and you call Kate and McKenzie."

Chatter and laughter filled the room as Bailey and Alex told the others about Yeller, Dude, and Rude.

"Yeah, funny, huh?" Alex said to McKenzie. "Bailey just comes up with these crazy names for people. It's a hoot!"

"Of course we'll be careful, Elizabeth," Bailey said. "We won't get close to those men. But I might take a few pictures with my watch."

"I'm going to learn to shear sheep tomorrow!" Alex smiled as she spoke to Kate.

"You should have seen us run when that dog was chasing us, Sydney," Bailey told her athletic friend. "You would have been proud!"

Soon both girls finished their conversations and

reported back to each other.

"I told Kate we loved the picture of her and Biscuit," Alex said.

"Sydney said to keep up the good running, and maybe we can be in the Olympics with her someday." Bailey giggled.

"McKenzie wondered why those men even have a dog." Alex yawned. "She said maybe they aren't as mean as we thought."

"They sure acted mean, and so did their dog," Bailey said. "I didn't see anything nice about any of them—except Yeller didn't seem to be threatening us."

"How's Elizabeth doing?"

"Good. She doesn't want us approaching those men. Too dangerous."

"Well, duh!" Alex said. "That's what I said earlier."

"I still plan to get some pictures of them though," Bailey said.

"If you can do it safely, I'm all for it."

"They sure would be handy in trying to identify Yeller, Dude, and Rude to see if they have anything to do with Gonzo's case."

"You can say that again." Alex saw Bailey's black eyes twinkle and a smile play at her mouth. "But don't."

"You know me too well." Bailey grinned then yawned. "I'm getting sleepy."

"It's been a big day."

"And tomorrow should be even bigger with all the

shearing." Bailey pulled her pajamas out of the dresser drawer.

"We'd better get to bed early so we'll be rested and ready for it."

"I plan to get some photos of those guys tomorrow after we're done shearing."

"If they're outside again," Alex added. "Seems like Dude and Rude like to keep Yeller in the house and out of sight."

"Yeah, it does," Bailey agreed, squeezing toothpaste onto her toothbrush. "But maybe we'll get lucky. Yeller may come up with a way to go out since he saw us."

The girls brushed their teeth and crawled into bed. Bailey took care to remove her camera watch and set it on the dresser; then she switched off the light.

"I just hope he's okay until we can figure out a way to help." Alex pulled the blanket up to her chin. "Don't forget to pray for him."

"And don't forget to pray for *us* to know the right thing to do," Bailey added. She turned on her side and snuggled into her pillow.

Outside, Shy barked from the sheep pasture. "Silly Shy," Bailey murmured.

Alex giggled, but the barking continued.

There was a sudden rustling outside the bedroom window, then a yell.

The girls bolted upright in bed, eyes wide.

CHAPTER 4

A Strange Place for a Message

Bailey and Alex held their breath, too afraid to speak. They sat still as stones waiting for whatever would happen next. Only their eyes moved as their gaze shifted alternately from each other to the window that sat squarely between their twin beds. Finally, Alex put her index finger to her lips and motioned Bailey out of bed. Trembling, Bailey crouched on the floor by Alex, and then they crawled to the window. Alex peeked over the second-story sill, which was only three feet from the floor. The moon shone brightly, washing the huge oak tree just outside the window with pale blue light.

Bolstering her courage, Bailey also poked her head cautiously over the sill so she could see into the dimly lit yard. "Look!" She pointed toward a grove of trees at the far side of the yard where a man limped toward the thicket.

"That's Yeller!" Alex whisper-yelled.

The injured man disappeared into the woods. Wide-eyed, Bailey stared at Alex.

"The yell we heard must have been Yeller, but what was the rustling just before that?" Bailey asked.

Alex put her face to the window again. "Look under the tree."

Bailey's eyes followed Alex's finger. A broken branch and fallen leaves littered the yard. "He climbed the tree and then fell out!"

"What do you think he was doing here?" Bailey licked her lips nervously.

"Maybe he was trying to get a message to us," Alex suggested, trying for an explanation that wouldn't give her nightmares.

Hoping to chase away her fear, Bailey flipped the light back on and sat on Alex's bed to sort out what had just happened. "But how did he know which window was ours?"

"Good question." Alex picked a hangnail on her left thumb.

"He had to have been watching the house, don't you think?"

Alex nodded, her eyes fearful.

"Maybe he's desperate to talk to us about helping him."

"I think we may need to tell someone about this," Alex said.

"No!" Bailey grabbed Alex's hand. "We can't! We'll never be able to solve the Gonzo case if we tell. They'll think it's too dangerous."

"Well, maybe it is!" Alex's nose turned red as if she were about to cry.

"Come on, Alex. You know how careful we are. We won't take any unnecessary risks."

Alex remained silent, head down.

"Please?" Bailey pleaded. "With cherries on top?"

A faint smile played at the edges of Alex's mouth.

"Come on. . .I see that smile," Bailey teased. "You want to say yes, don't you?"

Finally, Alex broke down and laughed. "You are too much!" She tickled Bailey. "You know I want to solve this mystery as much as you do, but it's pretty scary right now."

"That's half the fun of it!" Bailey's eyes gleamed.

"I guess you're right. I may be older than you, but I'm not braver!"

"You're brave enough. You were the first one to look out the window, remember?" Bailey yawned. "Wow. It's already ten o'clock. We're going to be beat in the morning."

"Yeah. We'd better try to get some sleep, though I'm wide awake after that scare." Alex shivered. "Morning will be here before we know it."

Shoulders drooping, Bailey dragged herself to the light switch, flipped it back off, and staggered back to bed. "I'm half asleep already." She stretched and snuggled back into her pillow.

"Good night, Bailey," Alex said.

"Good night."

The alarm blared a loud country love song at six o'clock, and the girls dragged themselves out of bed. They put on jeans and pulled sweatshirts over their T-shirts. After scarfing down breakfast, they met Uncle Nathan in the barn for a morning of sheep shearing.

"Morning!" Uncle Nathan greeted them over the noisy baaing of the sheep. "A nice crisp morning for shearing, huh?"

"It sure is!" Bailey rubbed her hands together. "But it will warm up nice by this afternoon."

"Guess what I heard on the local news last night?" Uncle Nathan and Shy had already brought several sheep from the pasture and penned them up in the barn.

"What?" Bailey asked.

"The annual sheep-shearing contest for kids is this Saturday at the state fairgrounds."

"Cool!" Bailey gave a thumbs-up.

"Yep. It's here in the newspaper this morning, too." Uncle Nathan snatched a rolled-up paper from his back pocket. "Says here there will be three age categories: nine to eleven years old, twelve to fourteen, and sixteen to eighteen."

"Will Brian be in it?" Bailey asked.

"Maybe," Uncle Nathan answered. "But I was thinking you might be interested in trying the nine- to eleven-year-old category. What do you say?"

"Me? Could I?" Bailey's dark eyes danced.

"I don't see why not. You've had a few summers to practice, and you can still work at it all week." Uncle Nathan patted her back. "I'd be proud to have you participate as part of my family."

"Wow! I'd love to!"

Alex grabbed Bailey's hands, and they both jumped up

and down. "I'm so excited for you! It'll be fun to see how fast you can get this week."

"I just have to remember not to rush 'cause I don't want to hurt the sheep." Bailey petted the ewe Uncle Nathan just brought from the pen. "Right, girl?"

"I'll do this one; then you do the next." Uncle Nathan reached for the shears.

"And Alex wants to have a try after that," Bailey added.

Uncle Nathan nodded and smiled at Alex. "Good girl. You can't let your fears get the best of you." He flipped the sheep onto its rump, its front legs up in the air, so it wouldn't struggle with him. Then he turned on the shears, running them along the sheep's body. Fleece dropped, and Uncle Nathan was done in no time.

Bailey giggled at the naked sheep.

"Now it's your turn, Bailey." Uncle Nathan returned the first sheep to its pen and came back with another. "Wait a minute. I need to get something." He handed Bailey the rope lead that circled the sheep's neck while he went to the house.

Uncle Nathan returned holding a stopwatch. "I'll help you turn the sheep onto its backside. Then we'll time you so we can have a record of your first training-day time and see how you improve by Saturday. Take your time. You don't have to rush. You'll just naturally get faster the more you do it."

"Okay. Tell me when to start." Bailey held the sheep firmly with one hand and the shears in the other.

"Ready. . .go!" Uncle Nathan watched his niece shear, his eyes moving back and forth from her to the watch.

"You're doing great, Bailey!" Alex encouraged over the buzz of the shears. "Keep it up!"

Bailey kept working intently. "Done!" she finally yelled.

Uncle Nathan stopped the watch. "Twenty-two minutes, forty-three seconds."

"That's awesome!" Alex hugged her friend.

"What's the time that won last year?" Bailey asked.

Uncle Nathan reached for the newspaper in his back pocket again and scanned the article. "In your age bracket, the winning time was twelve minutes, twenty seconds."

Bailey's face dropped. "You mean I have to cut my time almost in half?"

"Only if you want to win." Uncle Nathan grinned.

"You can do it, Bailey!" Alex's natural cheerleading spirit bubbled to the surface, and she did a backflip.

"With support like that, how can you lose?" Uncle Nathan laughed and put his hand on Bailey's shoulder. "And like I said, don't worry about the time. Just do your best. The time will take care of itself."

"I'll try." Bailey looked at Alex. "Your turn."

The color drained from Alex's face. Then she stomped her foot with determination. "I'm ready! No sheep is going to scare me!"

"Good for you!" Bailey led a sheep toward her friend while her uncle swept up the wool from the sheep she had just sheared.

Uncle Nathan leaned his broom against the barn wall and stepped in to sit the sheep on its rump for Alex.

"Now hold it like this." Bailey demonstrated how to hold the animal between her legs. "And flip this switch when you're ready to start."

Uncle Nathan stood close by. "We'll be right here to answer your questions and help you if you need it."

Alex turned on the shears. The sheep startled at the buzz but immediately calmed when the noise became constant.

Alex ran the shears down the stomach, sides, and back of the sheep. Wool fell like a blanket onto the cleanly swept floor. Soon she said, "How's that look?"

"Great!" Uncle Nathan answered. "Looks like you'll make a shearer after all!"

"Way to go, Alex! You did it!" Bailey helped her friend turn the sheep back onto its feet.

"I can't believe I just sheared a sheep!" Alex bounced up and down.

"Now, how about if you girls work on shearing the lambs and yearlings over there, and I'll handle the ewes and rams over here?" suggested Uncle Nathan. "I think you'll find shearing the smaller animals easier." He looked at Alex. "I'll turn the stopwatch over to you so you can check Bailey's time again after she's done a few."

Bailey and Alex moved about halfway down the barn where another set of electric shears hung from the ceiling. They decided they'd share the shears until Alex felt confident enough to handle her own shearing station. Then Bailey would move on down to the next set at the end of the barn. There were four shears in all, and Uncle Nathan said Brian would be out soon to help him with the ewes and rams.

Bailey sheared the first young sheep while Alex played with the lambs. Then they swapped places. After two hours, they had finished five lambs, and the morning had warmed up enough for the girls to shed their sweatshirts. Alex checked Bailey's time again and found she'd already taken two minutes off her time. They leaned against the sheep pen and admired their work. The lambs bleated woefully for their mothers.

"That's hard work!" Alex wiped sweat and dirt from her face with the bottom of her T-shirt.

"I know. Even the little ones take a lot of time." Bailey gulped a long drink of water. "I'll take the next one." She led a yearling from the pen and over to the shearing area. Alex stayed in the pen with the ones yet to be sheared.

Bailey began shearing the yearling's belly and was soon running the shears over the side of the young sheep. Strange dark markings appeared on its skin as the fleece fell to the floor. She turned it over to shear the other side. The same strange markings appeared on that side, too. They weren't spots like some of the sheep had. They were more like black lines. "Hey Alex!" she yelled over the noise of the shears. "Come take a look at this!"

Bailey shut off the shears. She set the lamb on its feet

and asked, "What do you make of these markings?"

Alex walked around the lamb to study them. "Weird!"

"They're on both sides." Bailey turned the sheep for her to see.

"Almost looks like writing," Alex said.

"That's what I thought, too."

"Let's walk him out to the sunlight so we can see better."

Bailey led the sheep out of the barn, squinting against the bright sun. The lamb jumped playfully in its warmth. "Hold still now," Bailey cooed as she crouched beside the animal and petted it. "We want to get a good look at you." She held the lamb firmly for Alex to inspect.

Alex stepped back and cocked her head. "Oh my goodness!"

"What?"

"It spells something!"

"What?" Bailey asked, excitement rising in her voice.

"It says, 'Help'!" Alex clapped her hand over her mouth when she checked out the other side. " 'Gonzo'! I think it says, 'Gonzo'!"

"No way!" Bailey said. "How could writing get under a sheep's fleece, much less something about Gonzo, which is a nickname I made up only yesterday!"

"I don't know, but I'm sure that's what it says," Alex insisted. "See for yourself. I'll hold the lamb."

The girls traded places, and Bailey studied the animal. She looked at it standing up, and then knelt. She squinted while she examined the lamb, shielding her eyes from the sun with her hand. "You're right." Bailey stood back up. "It definitely says, 'Help Gonzo.' But that doesn't make sense."

"We need to hide this lamb so no one else sees it." Alex glanced over her shoulder.

"Quick. In the pasture." Bailey led the lamb toward the gate. "Let's put all the sheared lambs back so no one wonders why they aren't all together. You go get a couple others, and I'll be there in a second to help you."

"I'm on it." Alex swung back toward the barn. At the pen, she took the rope leads off a nail on the wall and slid them over the lambs' heads. "Come on, let's go." The lambs resisted, loudly voicing their complaints, and Alex had to drag them a few feet before they gave up and started walking. "There, that's better," she soothed.

Bailey ran back to the barn, so deep in thought that she hardly noticed Alex pass. She carefully examined the remaining sheep to make sure they didn't have markings.

When the last lamb was back in the pasture, Bailey leaned against the fence, watching them caper around playfully, glad to be back home. The young lambs quickly nuzzled their mothers to nurse. "What do you think the message means?" she asked.

"It could read either 'Help Gonzo' or 'Gonzo help.' So it sounds like either Gonzo is asking for help or someone is asking for Gonzo's help. I suppose it makes most sense that it's a cry for help from Gonzo."

"Do you think this Gonzo is Marshall Gonzalez or someone else?" Bailey asked.

"Who knows?" Alex pulled a blade of grass to chew. "I guess we could ask around to see if there's anyone that goes by Gonzo around here."

"The other girls will go nuts when they hear this," Bailey said. "I'll snap a few pictures of our 'talking' lamb to send to them."

"Good idea. Maybe they'll see something we missed."

Bailey took several photos from different angles. "We'd better get back to the barn before Uncle Nathan wonders what happened to us. I still need to sweep up before you start on your next sheep."

The girls worked for two more hours but found no more mysterious writing.

Uncle Nathan turned off his shears and came by to check on their progress. "How you ladies doing?"

"Great! We've done twelve sheep." Bailey stood tall.

"Not bad for the first day." Uncle Nathan said. "You've had a long morning of shearing. Ready to call it a day?"

"As soon as we get these last few back to the pasture and sweep up. We already took the first few out earlier." Bailey looked down at her clothes. "I'm filthy! I need a shower!"

"Just shows you've been working hard, that's all." Uncle Nathan laughed and hugged her. "Good job, girls. You can have the rest of the day off."

Bailey smiled at Alex. "See! I told you he wouldn't make us work the whole day."

Alex laughed. "You'd better be quiet, or he might change his mind."

After the girls finished their work in the barn and showered, Bailey downloaded the pictures she took.

"You're getting better with that camera watch!" Alex watched the photos pop up on the computer screen. "Only two blurry ones this time—and that might be because the sheep were running around so much."

"Thanks. I held my arm against my body when I took the pictures so I'd be steadier. Maybe that helped."

"You got some pretty clear shots. Let's e-mail the other Camp Club members about this mysterious message."

"Okay," Bailey said. "And we have to tell them about Yeller falling from the tree outside our bedroom window last night."

"Right." Alex typed the note then pressed SEND, and off it went along with the picture attachments.

Elizabeth was quick to e-mail back, reminding them to be careful and that she was praying for them and their safety.

A knock sounded at the bedroom door. "Yes?" Bailey answered.

"It's me, Brian. Can I come in?"

Alex quickly closed her computer and looked at Bailey.

"Yeah, I guess." Bailey got up and opened the door. "What's up?"

"Did you guys see the weird markings on that sheep you sheared?" he asked.

CHAPTER 5

An Unexpected Assistant

Bailey decided to play dumb until she found out what Brian knew. "Weird markings? What are you talking about?"

"You *had* to have seen them!"

"What did they look like?" Alex asked innocently.

"They looked like words!" Brian's voice rose.

"Words?" Bailey's tone indicated she thought her cousin had gone stark raving mad. "What did they say?" She glanced at Alex. Alex had her hand over her mouth, trying to hide a grin.

Brian looked at the floor, seemingly embarrassed at what he was about to say. His thick, wavy black hair hung like a curtain around his face, "It said, uh, well, it said, 'Help Gonzo,' " he finally blurted.

"Gonzo? Who's that?" Bailey asked.

"Yeah, and why does he need help?" Alex added.

"I don't know!" Brian threw his hands up in frustration. "I just figured you had seen the words, too, so I came to see what you thought about them!"

Bailey and Alex's eyes met, and they burst out laughing.

"That's it! I'm leaving!" Brian reached for the doorknob.

"No! No!" Bailey gasped, regaining her composure. "We saw the markings. We were just having some fun with you, that's all."

"Yeah," Alex said. "Sorry if we took it too far."

"So you *did* see them. I knew it!" Brian raised a clenched fist. "What did you make of them?"

"I'd say that sheep must have had weird-looking parents." Bailey smirked. She didn't want to give too much information about their investigation until she knew if Brian could be trusted not to tell.

"You are impossible," Brian said to his little cousin through gritted teeth.

"Well, what did *you* make of them?" Bailey countered.

"I already told you what they looked like to me!" Brian growled. " 'Help Gonzo'!"

Alex gave Bailey a cautionary look then turned her eyes back to Brian. "We thought the same thing," she said quietly.

Brian's eyes lit up. "Really?" He stepped away from the door and moved toward the girls.

"Really," Bailey finally admitted.

"So I'm not going crazy!"

"Not today, anyway," Bailey teased.

"Why didn't you tell someone about the markings?" Brian asked.

"Did *you* tell someone?" Alex asked, suddenly wishing she'd kept her big mouth shut.

"Only you," Brian answered.

"You didn't tell your parents?" Bailey questioned.

"No. Why?"

Bailey and Alex exchanged looks and nodded.

Bailey spoke first. "Because we think we know who Gonzo might be, but we don't want anyone else to know until we're sure about what we think we know."

"Huh?" Brian's eyes glazed over a bit.

"Sit down," Alex suggested. "We'll explain."

Brian looked for a chair but only saw a pink beanbag. "I'm not sitting in that."

"Oh come on. It won't turn you into a girl," Bailey teased.

Brian hesitated. "You'd better keep this quiet." He pulled the feminine chair close to Bailey's bed where both girls sat. The beans whooshed when he plopped down, and Alex laughed out loud. "I'm warning you. . . ," Brian threatened, but Bailey saw a smile sneaking into his snarl.

Bailey and Alex alternately filled Brian in on who they thought Gonzo might be and what they'd discovered so far about the mystery. They left out the part about Yeller, Dude, and Rude, since they didn't know if the men really fit into the Gonzo mystery. Brian's dark eyes grew bigger with every detail.

"I can't believe it! You guys have only been here three days, and you're already working on a mystery the police haven't solved in seven years!" Brian shook his head.

"But you have to promise not to tell." Bailey pointed a menacing finger at Brian.

"I promise," Brian said.

"Cross your heart?" Alex pushed.

"Cross my heart." Brian made an *X* on his chest with his finger then leaned in. "So you'll keep me posted on any other clues you find?"

"Sure, if you want us to." Bailey nodded her head vigorously.

"You can't tell me all this and then leave me in the dark!" Brian's bright white smile lit up his face.

"Okay. We'll keep you posted," Alex promised.

"How do you think the writing got on the sheep?" Bailey asked.

"It isn't a normal brand, that's for sure," Brian said.

"Looked like a marker to me," Alex added.

"But it was so wide. Do they make markers that fat?" Bailey cocked her head. "And it would have to be permanent to withstand the weather."

"They make big permanent markers for writing on outdoor banners," Brian said.

"How big?" Alex asked.

"The biggest I've seen was probably about an inch wide." Brian held his finger and thumb about an inch apart to show them. "The spirit squad used them at school on posters for football games. And our vacation Bible school director at church used one to write on the banner for the church lawn."

"Good information, Brian," Alex said. "Anything else you know about the markers?"

"They smell horrible!" Brian laughed. "When we used them to make posters at school, our classroom smelled toxic for a couple of days!"

"Perfect!" Bailey clapped her hands.

"What do you mean?" Alex asked.

"We can smell the yearling to see if it has any leftover marker smell!"

"I doubt that it would now." Brian shook his head. "Who knows how long ago that message was written? Besides, markers would be bad for the sheep."

"It's still a clue we need to check out," Bailey insisted.

"She's right," Alex agreed. "A good detective leaves no clue unturned."

"Don't you mean 'leaves no rock unturned'?" Now it was Brian's turn to tease.

"Whatever." Alex smiled. "Let's just turn it over, whatever it is!"

"Brian, do you know where those sheep came from?" Bailey asked.

"Hard to know for sure," her cousin answered. "We bought a lot of sheep at auctions last year to stock up our herds. They came from several different ranches in the area."

"Any way we could find out?" Alex asked.

"I think my dad keeps a record book of when sheep are bought and which farms they come from."

Bailey gave him a you've-got-to-be-kidding look. "A record book?"

"I know. Dad's too old-fashioned to use a computer spreadsheet," Brian answered. "Anyway, he also puts tiny tags on each of the sheep's ears to identify them. He may even record how many sheep he gets at each auction." Brian paused. "The problem is, we won't know for sure which ones came from which farm."

"That info sure would help us narrow down the possibilities, though," Bailey said, excitement rising in her voice.

"Brian, do you think you could get a list of auctions and farms your dad bought from in the past year?" Alex asked. "We can check out each one to see if it's tied in any way to Gonzo."

"I'm not sure, but I could try." Brian rubbed his chin. "I'll have to snoop around my dad's office to find his record book. It's a mess in there!"

"Just be careful. Don't get into any trouble." Bailey's eyes narrowed with concern.

"I won't. Don't worry." Brian thought another minute. "You know, Gonzo could be one of the seasonal migrant workers."

"You think so?" Alexis asked.

"Maybe," Brian said. "Gonzalez is a pretty common name among them."

"Why would one of them need help?" Bailey wondered aloud.

"Good question," Brian responded. "Many of them are pretty poor."

"Seems like an odd way to get help with money." Bailey twisted her mouth.

"Especially if you have children to feed," Alex added. "You'd want quicker results than hoping someone saw your message months later during shearing season."

"I still think we shouldn't rule it out," Brian said. "Never leave a clue unturned." He grinned at Alex.

Alex returned the smile. "You're right. You just might make a good detective after all."

"By the way, how'd the shearing go today?" Brian asked.

"Alex was awesome!" Bailey bragged. "She sheared as many sheep as I did!"

"Only because we were trading off," Alex added modestly. "If I'd been shearing at my own station, you would have done lots more."

"I knocked two minutes off my starting time." Bailey held up two fingers.

"So you're definitely going to compete this weekend?" Brian asked.

"I'm pretty sure. We'll see how much faster I can get first."

Brian looked at Alex. "What about you? Are you going to try it?"

"Me?" Alex squeaked. "You've got to be kidding! This was only my first day of shearing in my whole life. I don't think I'm quite ready."

"Are you going to be in the competition, Brian?" Bailey asked.

"I competed the last few years. I'm not sure if I'll enter again this year." Brian flexed his muscles. "Although I've been training and am a lot stronger now. These guns could really handle those sheep this year!" He patted his right bicep, and all three of them laughed.

"Brian!" Uncle Nathan's voice boomed up the stairs.

"I'm coming, Dad!" Brian jumped up from the beanbag chair. "I've got to get back to work or Dad will get suspicious. Must be nice having the rest of the afternoon off!" he teased. Then he added, "I'll let you know if I find anything about the auctions in his records."

"Thanks, Brian!" Bailey pushed the beanbag back to the wall as her cousin left the room, then sat back on her bed again.

"He could be a huge help with this case," Bailey said.

"I just hope we didn't give him too much information too soon."

"I think we can trust Brian. He seemed excited to be included in the secret, don't you think?"

"Yeah, he seemed excited," Alex agreed. "I just hope he is excited for the right reasons."

"What do you mean?"

"He might just want to use the information to get us in trouble or something. Don't forget, he's a boy!"

Bailey shook her head. "I doubt it. Brian's not like that."

"He did seem pretty sincere, didn't he?"

"Yeah, and if he can get those records of Uncle Nathan's, that will be worth a lot even if he doesn't do another thing!"

Bailey's cell phone rang, startling the girls. She looked at the display window before flipping it open. "Hi, Kate!"

Alex watched her friend intently as she talked.

"Uh-huh. . . . Really? You're kidding!" Bailey's eyes widened.

"What?" Alex whispered impatiently, unable to contain her curiosity.

Bailey held up her index finger to Alex and listened. She scribbled some notes on a pad of paper on her nightstand and said, "Great work, Kate. Let us know if you find out anything else. Okay. Yeah, I'll tell her. Bye."

"What? What'd she find out?" Alex's questions exploded out of her like lava from an active volcano.

"First of all, she said to tell you hi." Bailey smiled sweetly, not rushing into the information Alex was dying to hear.

"Hi, already! Now tell me what she said!"

"Okay. She did some Internet research, which she said was pretty tough because there were a gazillion listings for people named Gonzalez. But there weren't many with the first name of Marshall. She was able to narrow it down and found out that our Marshall Gonzalez was born in Sinoloa, Mexico. He grew up the son of a poor shrimp fisherman. However, his grandpa raised sugar cane and was very wealthy."

"Wait a minute, if his grandpa was wealthy, why was his dad so poor?" Alex asked.

"Good question. We'll have to look into that."

"What else?" Alex prompted.

"When Grandpa Sugar Cane died, he left his fortune to his only grandson, Marshall Gonzalez."

"Aha! So that's who he inherited his money from. Go on."

"That's as far as she's gotten so far," Bailey said with a sigh.

"Man! She really knows how to leave a girl hanging,

doesn't she?" Alex laughed. "She did great getting that much information to us already. I know she'll dig up more."

"Hey, I've got an idea!" Bailey sat up straight. "Let's conference call the Camp Club Girls and give them all the updates. We can get their takes on this new info Kate just gave us."

"Great idea!" Alex scooted right next to Bailey so she'd be closer to the phone.

Bailey called each girl individually then conferenced them in together. She put the phone on speaker so she and Alex could both hear.

"Syd, can you hear me?" she asked.

"I can hear you," Sydney answered.

"Elizabeth, are you there?"

"I'm right here," she replied.

"How about you, McKenzie?"

"I read you loud and clear!" McKenzie giggled.

"Kate, can you hear us?"

"Biscuit and I are all ears." Kate's voice gave away her smile.

"Alex and I are on my speaker phone, so we're both here, too." Bailey held the phone between her and Alex. "Kate, why don't you tell the others the information you've found out so far about Gonzo."

The other girls laughed at the nickname Bailey had come up with for Marshall Gonzalez.

Kate repeated what she'd already told Bailey and Alex.

"Sounds like jealousy may be a motive for this case,

since Gonzalez is the only heir to his grandfather's money," McKenzie said.

"Do we know if other grandchildren were left out of Grandpa's will?" asked Alex.

"Not yet," Kate said. "He was the only grandson, but there could have been granddaughters. I'll check that out, and also try to find out if Gonzo's father was still living when his father died. He could have been pretty mad to have been left out of the will, too."

"Jealousy can cause people to do things they wouldn't do otherwise," Elizabeth piped in. "Proverbs 6:34 says, 'For jealousy arouses a husband's fury, and he will show no mercy when he takes revenge.' I'd say the same is true for anyone, not just husbands. Gonzo's family could have been very angry as well as jealous, and taken revenge, which could be why we have a missing man!"

"Good point, Elizabeth," Sydney said. "I think I'll research the sugar cane and shrimping industry to see if I can learn any helpful clues from that."

"Good thinking, Syd," Alex said. "Hey, guess what, you guys? We have someone else helping us with the case now." Alex told them about Brian and that he was investigating the Curly Q's purchasing records for them.

"You're sure we can trust him?" Elizabeth asked.

"I'm sure," Bailey answered. "Let's talk again in two days to see what new information has come to light. If we have any big breaks, we can always talk sooner."

"Like if Bailey learns to shear a sheep in two minutes

or less and sets a new world record!" Alex laughed and explained to the others that their youngest friend was going to be in a shearing competition this Saturday.

"That'll be awesome!" McKenzie said. "I wonder if Biscuit would make a good sheepdog."

"I wish we could all come to watch." Elizabeth's gentle voice conveyed her remorse.

"We'll let you know how it goes," Bailey assured them. "In the meantime, let's keep working on the case, and we'll talk again in a couple days."

"Sounds good to me," McKenzie said.

"Me, too!" added Kate.

"Woof!" Biscuit barked in the background, and the girls all laughed.

"Guess we have Biscuit's approval, too," Kate said.

"And remember, we only have four more days until Alex and I go back home," Bailey reminded them.

"I wish I was as fast at solving mysteries as I am on the track!" Sydney joked.

The girls said their good-byes and hung up.

"Come on," Bailey said. "Let's get out of here for a while. It's a beautiful day!"

Alex was off the bed in a flash. They opened the bedroom door and immediately heard voices downstairs. They stopped to listen before going down.

Uncle Nathan's voice rose. "Brian! What are you doing in my office?"

Another Message

Bailey clapped her hand over her mouth. How could Brian be so careless after she had trusted him with their investigation secrets?

"Dad!" Brian's voice cracked.

"What are you doing in here?" Uncle Nathan repeated.

Bailey crept silently down the stairs with Alex close behind. They stopped three steps from the bottom where they could see into the office. They sat to watch the unfolding horror show.

"I was looking for something," Brian hedged.

"I gathered that." Uncle Nathan paused. "Are you going to tell me what it is you're looking for?"

Brian lowered his eyes. "I was trying to remember which farms we bought sheep from at the last few auctions. I couldn't remember, so I was going to look it up."

Uncle Nathan gazed at his son without a smile. Brian met his father's eyes squarely, holding a stare for a second before Uncle Nathan's face softened. He put a hand on his son's shoulder. "So you're taking an interest in the family business, huh?"

"Yeah, I guess," Brian replied, relief flooding his features.

"I've always hoped you'd want to learn more about the business side of sheep farming, rather than just the animal care." Uncle Nathan opened a desk drawer and pulled out a spiral-bound black book.

"This is my ledger," he explained to Brian. "In it I keep records of which auctions I attend, which farms I buy sheep from, and what I pay." He handed the book to his son. "I know I should put all this in the computer, but I just haven't made the switch yet. Maybe I'm just too old-fashioned."

Brian held the softcover book, flipping through its lined pages of columns and rows. "It has a lot of writing in it. How long have you been keeping track of all this?"

"Since I bought the farm. About seven years."

"Wow. Can I borrow this to do some research?"

"What are you researching?"

Alex inhaled sharply. Bailey grabbed her friend's hand and squeezed as they waited for Brian's reply.

"I want to try to figure out which sheep came from which farms so I can see if their markings are similar. You know, to see if sheep have any family resemblances like people do."

Uncle Nathan's eyebrows shot up, and he grinned. "Oh, I see. Like a genetic engineer!" He smacked his son on the back. "Sure! Look all you want. I'd better start saving my money for your high-priced education!"

The proud father strutted toward the office door but then stopped and turned back to Brian. "But son, next time you need something, please ask me for it instead of snooping. It doesn't look good when you do that."

Brian laughed. "Sure, Dad. Sorry. Hey, maybe I could enter this stuff into a spreadsheet on the computer for you. It would take some time, but I know how to do it."

Uncle Nathan's face lit up. "Sure! That would be a tremendous help. Thanks!"

Bailey and Alex heard the screen door slam as Uncle Nathan went back outside. They hurried into the office.

"That was too close for comfort!" Bailey searched Brian's face for any hint of remorse.

"You said you were going to be careful," Alex accused.

"I *was* careful! I got out of the mess, didn't I? And I even got permission to look through the record book." Brian held up the ledger.

Bailey sighed. "Yeah, you did. Sorry. I was just scared, that's all."

"Don't be such a worrywart." Brian scowled. "You're worse than my mom."

"Well, this is our investigation, and we've worked hard on it already!" Bailey crossed her arms dramatically and frowned. "We just don't want it getting messed up by one careless move—or person!"

"It's okay, Bailey." Alex patted her friend on the back. "Brian didn't mean to upset you, did you, Brian?" She looked pointedly at him.

"No, of course not."

"I'm sure he'll be more careful in the future. And he did

a fabulous job getting the book quickly so we have lots of time to look it over."

"We? I never said you could see it," Brian said.

Now Alex stood straight, glaring at Brian. "What did you say?"

"I told my dad *I* wanted to look at it. I never said *you* could look at it. It's private business."

"Brian Chang, you give me that book!" Bailey charged at him.

Brian laughed and held it up higher than her reach. "I'll look at it and then tell you what I find out. That way we can keep everyone happy. If my dad asks me if I showed it to anyone, I can honestly say no."

Bailey growled, her eyes flaming, then collapsed in a chair. "Fair enough. We don't want Uncle Nathan to get mad at you."

"But you have to promise to tell us everything you find that might relate to the mystery," Alex said.

"I promise."

"Hope to die?" Bailey prodded.

"Not particularly, but if it will make you feel better, then I guess." Brian grinned.

Bailey opened her mouth to speak but was interrupted by her cousin.

"And sure, I'd love to stick a needle in my eye, too, while I'm at it!"

Bailey laughed. "Okay. I'm happy now. But remember, this is top secret!"

"Like you'd let me forget." Brian playfully shoved Bailey. "I need to get back to the barn. I'll keep you posted."

●—●—●

The next morning, Bailey and Alex arose early for their second day of shearing. Bailey wrapped her arms around herself in the crisp air as the sheep bleated their greetings. She was happy to see that Alex was much more at ease with the animals than the day before. She went right into the pasture to talk to them. Little Bow baaed her greeting to the girls, and Alex bent down and hugged her neck. Bailey joined her and immediately spotted the lamb with the message on it. "Let's see if it smells like marker," she suggested.

"I don't know if we'll be able to smell anything but sheep with all these others around." Alex held her nose.

They pushed their way through the herd to the yearling. Its mother stood between them and her baby.

"It's okay, Mama," Bailey cooed. "We aren't going to hurt your baby." She held out her hand for the sheep to nuzzle while Alex moved around to the other side of the lamb.

Quickly, Alex knelt and sniffed the markings. "All I can smell is sheep. Let's take it further away from the others and try again."

"I don't think his mama will allow that." Bailey tried to distract the ewe, but she moved closer to her lamb.

"You're a good mother," Bailey told her. "We'll let you be."

"You girls ready to get started?" Uncle Nathan called from the barn.

"Coming!" Bailey yelled.

Bailey and Alex took up their work, each at her own shearing station today. Uncle Nathan had put several lambs in pens for them to start on. The girls sheared in silence for about an hour; then Bailey heard Alex yell. She flipped off her shears. "What did you say?"

"Come here!" Alex shouted. Her arm waved Bailey over.

"Just a minute. I've got to finish up here first." Bailey turned the shears back on and quickly completed the job. She led the newly shorn lamb back to its pen and joined Alex.

"What's up?"

"I think we have another message." Alex pointed at the lamb she was shearing, tightening her grip on the rope around its neck. "Look."

Bailey studied the strange black streaks. "I can't read it." She tilted her head to get another angle.

"Let me finish shearing it, and we'll see if the other side says anything," Alex said. "Maybe it will help us figure out what this side says."

Alex ran the shears along the side of the sheep. The thick fleece dropped to the barn floor, uncovering more black streaks. "Yep. There's something here, too." Alex turned off the shears and showed Bailey.

"Looks like it starts with a *B*." Bailey examined the lamb closely, running her hand over its marked skin. "Let's take her out to pasture so we can see it in the sunlight. I'll bring another one, too, to avoid suspicion."

The pair coaxed the noisy lambs out of the barn and

into the bright sun. "Come on." Bailey pulled on the rope lead. "You can come out here where Bow is." Bailey put her lamb back in the pasture then tried to read the message on the young sheep Alex held. " 'Bundle'?" Bailey guessed at the word. " 'Bridle'? I'm not sure. You try."

She and Alex traded places. Alex stared at the writing, not saying anything. She walked around and looked at it from all angles. " 'Brindle'?" She shrugged her shoulders. "I don't know if that's even a word, but that's what it looks like to me."

"Take a look at the other side now and see what you think." Bailey turned the lamb around.

Alex gazed at its side. " 'Branch.' "

"Are you sure?" Bailey asked.

"Not completely, but it's the best I can come up with."

" 'Brindle Branch.' "

"Or 'Branch Brindle,' " Alex offered.

"Maybe it's not 'branch,' but 'ranch.'"

Alex looked at the writing again. "No, it definitely starts with a *B*."

"I wonder what it could mean."

"I think brindle might be an animal color. Seems like I heard that word when I was watching a dog show on TV. We'll have to look it up when we get back in the house."

"Let's hurry up and finish shearing so we can check this out." Bailey pointed her camera watch at the lamb bearing the message and snapped a few pictures.

After they finished their last few lambs, they returned

all the sheep to the pasture and returned to the barn.

"Uncle Nathan! We're done!" Bailey yelled over the buzz of the shears.

Uncle Nathan stopped his work and smiled. "You're done, huh? You must be getting pretty fast shearing those lambs. I'll have to bring more in for you tomorrow!" He laughed his big, hearty laugh.

"So can we be done working for today?" Bailey smiled and batted her eyes at her uncle.

"How can I say no to those sparkling brown eyes? Go on!" Uncle Nathan shooed them out of the barn with a wave of his hand.

Bailey gave Uncle Nathan a quick peck on the cheek. "You're the best!" She and Alex turned and raced back to the house, eager to investigate the latest message.

Alex opened her laptop and went to her online dictionary. "B-r-i-n-d-l-e." She typed in the word. "Here it is. 'Brindle or brindled: gray or tawny brown with darker streaks, patches, or spots.' "

"I've never seen a branch look like that," Bailey said. "What could 'Brindle Branch' mean?"

"Let's go outside and look at the trees. Maybe one will look more brindled than the others and give us a clue."

As the pair strolled the grounds of the Curly Q, they kept their eyes on the trees but saw nothing unusual.

"Let's go look over by the grove of trees where we saw Yeller disappear the other night," Bailey suggested. "There are more trees to study there."

In the grove, they spied a variety of trees. Some had rough bark, and others were smooth. The colors ranged from dark brown to ruddy red to almost white, but none looked patchy or streaked.

"I can't imagine what kind of tree would look like that," Bailey said.

"We'll just have to keep our eyes open from now on. Maybe we'll spot one that matches the description in the dictionary."

"What are you looking at?"

Bailey jumped, and Alex inhaled sharply.

"Brian! You scared us!" Bailey scolded her cousin. "You pop up in the weirdest places!"

"I could say the same thing about you."

"How'd you find us out here?" Alex asked.

"I saw you pass the barn. Not much out this way but the old grove." Brian looked around. "So what are you doing?"

"Investigating trees." Bailey looked up at the canopy of branches.

"That sounds like a good time." Brian patted his mouth as he yawned dramatically.

"Brian, we found another sheep with a message on it."

Brian's yawn ended abruptly and his eyes widened. "You're joking. What'd it say?"

"Brindle Branch," Alex said.

"Brindle Branch?" Brian repeated.

"Yeah. Any idea what it could mean?" Bailey asked.

"Not really." Brian scratched his head. "Sounds like it

would have something to do with a tree."

"That's what we thought."

"I'll have to think about it." Brian looked at the trees around them. "I was just getting ready to drive into town. Want to come?"

Bailey looked at Alex and shrugged. "I guess so. I've never ridden with you since you've been old enough to drive. Maybe we'll spy a brindle tree along the way."

"I'll tell Dad you're going with me." Brian ran to the barn while the girls piled into the car. He returned and climbed in behind the wheel. "Buckle up!"

"All set." Bailey sat in the backseat and Alex in the front.

Brian slowly pulled forward and onto the country road. "I have to pick up a few groceries for my mom. The Historical Society isn't far from there. Want me to drop you off? Maybe you can get some clues to your mystery."

"Yeah!" Alex said. "Maybe we'll find out more about Marshall Gonzalez or his family."

Brian turned onto Washington Street and parked in front of an old building with a sign that read: PEORIA HISTORICAL SOCIETY.

"I'll pick you up in an hour. I've got my cell phone if you need me to come get you sooner."

"Okay, thanks." Bailey climbed out of the backseat, and she and Alex marched up the steps to the main entrance.

"This place looks old," Alex said.

Bailey used all her weight to pull open the oversize wood door.

They each paid the suggested two-dollar donation and then went through a turnstile leading into the museum. The first thing they saw was an old, yellowed map of Peoria hanging on a wall in a glass case. It had brown lettering showing what the area had looked like before it was developed into a bustling town. Farmland covered much of the landscape, which the caption said the Illini Indians originally inhabited.

Bailey looked closely at the map, reading off the names of the rivers and creeks. "Alex! It says, 'Brindle Creek'!"

"No way. Where?"

Bailey pointed to a small creek that ran between acres of farmland.

"Unbelievable!"

"The map's so old I can't tell where the creek's located in relation to where the Curly Q is now."

"Me either," Alex said. "Let's keep looking. Maybe we'll find another clue."

Bailey and Alex split up and looked at two more maps, each more current than the last.

"Here it is!" Bailey called to Alex, who came rushing over. "Brindle Creek runs right between the Curly Q and that run-down house where Yeller, Dude, and Rude live."

"It must be the creek you were telling me about," Alex said. "Didn't you know what it was called?"

"That one's been called Woolly Creek for as long as I can remember, because of all the sheep farms surrounding it."

"Maybe it's not the same one then," Alex said

thoughtfully. "But it sure looks like it on the map."

"Or maybe the name changed over the years as sheep farmers moved in."

"Could be."

"Can I help you girls?"

Bailey turned and saw a plump, gray-haired woman with crinkles around her gentle green eyes. Her name tag indicated she was the museum curator.

"Yes," Bailey said. "We were wondering if this Brindle Creek still exists."

"Yes, it does. It runs along the same path, though it is much smaller than it used to be."

"Does it still go by the same name?" Alex asked.

"Oh no. It changed with the times, as most things do. Its name was changed to Woolly Creek about twenty years ago when the sheep industry took off in that area."

Bailey grinned at Alex, who gave her a thumbs-up.

"Thank you," Bailey said. "You've been very helpful."

"If I can answer any other questions, feel free to ask," the curator said warmly.

"Is it okay if I take a few pictures of these maps with my cell phone?" Alex asked.

"Certainly."

Alex snapped a picture of each map showing Brindle Creek. "We can send these to the Camp Club Girls when we get home."

"At least we have more to go on than we did a couple hours ago," Bailey said.

"Yeah," Alex agreed. "We didn't even know what *brindle* meant, and now we have a map showing us where it is!"

"Now if we could only figure out how it might fit into our mystery."

CHAPTER 7

Held Captive?

The next morning, Brian sauntered into the kitchen as Bailey and Alexis ate breakfast. He spread strawberry jam on his two pieces of toast, poured a big glass of milk, and sat down at the table. "Dad's already at the pasture bringing sheep into the barn, and Mom's at work," he said. "Here's what I found out from my dad's record book. We bought sheep from three different farms last year."

"Which ones?" Bailey asked around a mouthful of cereal.

"Hazelwood Sheep Farms, Hollyhock Acres, and Whitestone Ranch."

"Do you know where any of them are?" Alex asked.

"Their addresses were in the record book." Brian smiled proudly.

"Which one is closest?" Bailey wiped her mouth with the sleeve of her sweatshirt.

"It looks like Hazelwood Sheep Farms is closest, but I couldn't be sure from the address."

"Great. We can research it and find out." Alex looked at the clock. "Let's finish eating and get out to the barn."

"Yeah," Bailey agreed. "We need to check my shearing time again today."

"How's that going?" Brian asked.

"Pretty good. I'm down to eighteen minutes, twelve seconds."

"Way to go! You only need to trim five minutes, fifty-two seconds to match last year's winning time."

"And it's only Wednesday." Alex carried her bowl to the sink. "You still have three days to practice before Saturday's competition. If you keep knocking two minutes off each day, you'll beat last year's time easily!"

Brian wiped his mouth with his napkin, tossed it into the trash, and gulped down the last of his milk. "I'll go on out to see if Dad needs any help. See you out there!"

Bailey whipped out her phone. "I'm going to text Sydney to see if she can research Hazelwood Sheep Farms for us."

"Maybe we'll get an answer by the time we're done shearing today."

"That would be great." Bailey texted the message and sent it to Sydney, then put her phone back in her jeans pocket. "We only have three days left to solve this. Do you think we can get it done by Saturday?"

"Of course! We get more information every day!"

Shy scrambled across the yard to greet them. Bailey bent and scratched the dog's head. "I guess Uncle Nathan must have all the sheep already penned, or Shy would still be out there helping round them up."

Bailey took her place at her shearing station. "Let me know if you uncover anything interesting." She winked at Alex.

"You got it!" Alex moved to her spot and started working on a small black lamb.

The shears hummed along with the flies creating a buzzing symphony. Fleece dropped silently to the cement floor. Sheep baaed their complaints. The swish of brooms sweeping wool from the barn floor added rhythm.

Soon Bailey led her fourth lamb to the shearing floor, sat it on its rump, and ran the shears along its body. Black streaky marks appeared with each stroke. Another word! Bailey sheared faster, revealing letter after letter. H-e-l-d. She looked at Alex who was working, head down, on her own yearling. Quickly Bailey turned the sheep and sheared the other side. More letters; these were closer together and harder to read. Bailey again glanced toward Alex and caught her eye. She waved her over.

Alex returned her lamb to its pen and rushed to Bailey's station.

"Look!" Bailey said. "Another message. This side says, 'Held,' but I'm not sure about the other side." She flipped the lamb over for Alex to see.

Alex sounded out the word slowly as she read it. "Cap-tain?"

"Doesn't seem like that would be right." Bailey scrunched up her face. "Try again."

Alex stared at the lamb. "The letters are so close it's

hard to tell where one starts and the other stops." She studied the writing again. "C-a-p-t. That much I'm sure of. Maybe the last part is i-v-e."

"C-a-p-t-i-v-e. Captive! Alex, that's it!" Bailey squealed. The lamb squirmed. "Okay, baby. Let's go outside so we can take your picture."

Alex slipped a rope lead around the neck of the lamb Bailey held and got another lead to go on another lamb. She and Bailey led the animals out to pasture after snapping some photos of the mysterious writing.

"This is unbelievable!" Alex said. "I wonder how many other messages we'll find."

"I don't know. But I think we need to put all the words together that we've found so far to see if they say something as a group or if they're only individual messages."

"Yeah, let's do that after we're done. How many more sheep do you have left to shear?" Alex asked.

"Three. How about you?"

"Five."

"How about if you time my next one? Then when I finish my last one, I'll help you finish yours."

"Deal." Alex grabbed the stopwatch off a nail hook and waited for Bailey to get set up.

"Ready. . .set. . .go!" Alex started the clock, and Bailey started shearing. "You're doing great, Bailey! You're going to break your old record at this rate!"

"Done!" Bailey shouted minutes later.

Alex punched the stopwatch. "Fifteen minutes, forty-two

seconds!" Alex whooped. "Your best time yet! How did you do that so fast?"

"I pretended I saw a new message under the fleece and hurried to uncover it!"

Alex laughed. "Good strategy."

"I cut more than two minutes off my time!" Bailey hugged the naked lamb.

"You'll win that competition, I just know it," Alex said.

"Then I could get my picture in the newspaper!"

Alex beamed at her friend. "You'll be a star one way or another, even if it's not in theater, though I'm sure you'll make it there, too." The girls finished shearing the lambs and returned them to the pasture.

"I've got an idea," Bailey said. "Let's line up the sheep that have messages and take a picture of all three of them together."

"We'll need to take a picture of both sides to get all the words."

The girls gathered the lambs. Bailey tried to get two lambs to stand sideways by the other. "Can you hold all three of the leads and keep them in place while I take the picture?"

"I'll try, but hurry," Alex said. "They won't stay like this for long."

Bailey handed the leads to Alex and rushed in front of the lambs. She snapped pictures from that side and then the other. "They weren't perfectly lined up, but I think I got the words in all the shots."

They returned the sheep to the pasture. The lambs leaped with joy, clearing the ground with all four feet. Bow bleated a welcome to her newly shorn friends, her red bow sagging. Mama sheep baaed wildly and rushed to find their babies.

"Let's go see how they turned out." Alex took off at a run toward the house, with Bailey close behind.

"Wait!" Bailey stopped. "My phone's vibrating. Maybe it's Sydney." Bailey pulled her phone from her pocket and read the text.

HAZELWOOD FARMS IS A HALF MILE AWAY FROM YOU AND ON THE OTHER SIDE OF A CREEK.

Bailey looked at Alex wide-eyed. "Just across the creek? That's where Yeller, Dude, and Rude were!"

"That can't be right." Alex shook her head. "I didn't see any sheep over there."

"Maybe they keep them somewhere else. Or maybe they sold them all."

"Hmm. Interesting." Alex looked toward the old house. "Let's take a walk in that direction this afternoon."

Back at the house, Bailey downloaded her photos onto Alex's computer. "I think I'll write each word of the message on note cards. Then we can rearrange them and see what we get."

"Good idea." Alex dug in her backpack. "I think I have some note cards in here somewhere. Ah. Here they are." She handed the cards to Bailey.

"The first lamb said, 'Help Gonzo.' " Bailey wrote HELP

on one card and GONZO on another.

"The second one said, 'Brindle Branch,' " Alex said.

Bailey wrote the words on the cards. "And today's lamb said, 'Held captive.' " After writing the final words, Bailey laid the cards out in front of them. " 'HELP GONZO BRINDLE BRANCH HELD CAPTIVE.' Doesn't make much sense this way."

Alex rearranged the cards. " 'HELP GONZO HELD CAPTIVE BRINDLE BRANCH.' That's better."

"Seems like Gonzo's being held captive at Brindle Branch, wherever that is!"

"Now all we have to do is figure out that piece of the puzzle." Alex wrapped a curl around her finger and bit her lower lip.

"Do you really think this could be Marshall Gonzalez?" Bailey asked.

"Even if it isn't, this Gonzo needs our help."

"True. He must be desperate to send messages on sheep."

"This Gonzo must have been held captive since last shearing season to be able to write his messages on freshly shorn sheep."

"Good point," Bailey agreed. "Many of the farmers shear their sheep twice a year. That must be the case wherever this Gonzo is, because the lambs he wrote them on are only a year old. I doubt that he would have written on a newborn lamb. The mother never would have allowed that."

"So Gonzo probably wrote his messages about six months ago. He's been a hostage for at least six months!"

"How could anyone be held that long without someone knowing about it?" Bailey asked.

"We need to get the other Camp Club Girls in on this. Do you think we should do another conference call?"

"Yes. We have a lot to cover with them since we talked yesterday." Bailey got her phone out and started conferencing in the other girls.

Alex jotted down a few notes to help keep their meeting on track.

"Can you all hear me?" Bailey asked after patching in the last one.

"Kate here. I read you loud and clear."

"This is Sydney. I hear you."

"Me, too; it's Elizabeth,"

"McKenzie? You there?" Alex asked.

"I'm here," she answered.

Bailey heard Biscuit bark. "Biscuit hears you, too!" Kate said, and they all laughed.

"I'm here, too, so I guess we're ready to get started." Bailey cleared her throat. "Alex and I have uncovered some pretty interesting clues since we last talked, but we need your help researching them."

"Bailey and I found two more lambs with messages on them."

Bailey smiled at Alex as they listened to the girls gasp.

"What'd the new messages say?" Sydney asked.

"Alex's message said, 'Brindle Branch.' The letters were written in all capitals like the first message.

"And mine said, 'Held captive,' again in all capitals." Bailey licked her lips.

"We rearranged the words of all three messages today, and we believe they were meant to be read together. We think they should read, 'Help Gonzo held captive at Brindle Branch.' "

"Wow!" McKenzie said. "That's unbelievable."

"So how can we help?" Elizabeth asked.

"We went to the Historical Society yesterday to see if we could find a place called Brindle Branch," Alex said. "The closest we came was finding a Brindle Creek on an old map. It's the same creek that runs right behind the Curly Q, but now it goes by the name Woolly Creek."

"I took pictures of the map and will send those to you electronically," Bailey said. "We're wondering, if it is Gonzalez, how could a grown man be held captive so long without escaping? He had to have written the notes on the lambs at least six months ago when they were last sheared. Apparently he's allowed to go outside by himself."

"That's odd," McKenzie said. "You'd think he could run off if he was alone outside."

"I'll look into that," Kate offered. "I read something recently that may help."

"Great. Thanks, Kate." Alex looked at her notes. "We wonder if Marshall Gonzalez began sheep farming before he disappeared. That would make sense, since the messages are written on sheep. But if he were still in that business, someone else would probably have to be tending his sheep for him if he's being held hostage."

"Not an easy task," Elizabeth said. "Sheep know their shepherd's voice and won't follow anyone else. Their whole existence relies on the shepherd's care. Wait a minute. Let me read you something from my Bible."

Bailey heard the rustling of pages through the phone.

"Here it is, John 10:2–5. Listen to this." Elizabeth cleared her throat. " 'The man who enters by the gate is the shepherd of his sheep. The watchman opens the gate for him, and the sheep listen to his voice. He calls his own sheep by name and leads them out. When he has brought out all his own, he goes on ahead of them, and his sheep follow him because they know his voice. But they will never follow a stranger; in fact, they will run away from him because they do not recognize a stranger's voice.' " Elizabeth paused. Bailey guessed she was setting down her Bible. "That's why I say it wouldn't be easy for someone else to step in and take over the care of someone else's sheep."

"Interesting," McKenzie said slowly. "So if sheep don't take kindly to following strangers, then maybe Gonzo's kidnapping was an inside job, done by someone the sheep already knew."

"I suppose that's possible," Sydney said. "But why would someone kidnap their own friend?"

"That's easy," McKenzie said. "Money."

"She answered that awfully fast, don't you think, girls?" Alex said. "We'd better not get too rich, or she might kidnap *us*!"

Laughter filled the phone lines.

"We also found out," Bailey said, "that Uncle Nathan bought sheep from three different farms at auctions last year—Hazelwood Sheep Farms, Hollyhock Acres, and Whitestone Ranch. We're going to check them out to see if we can come up with any clues about which farm the sheep with messages might have come from. We had Sydney check out the farm locations earlier today, and she found out that Hazelwood is only a half mile from the Curly Q, so we'll start there."

"Good plan," Sydney said.

"Now, just to be fair, we should mention that Brian told us Gonzalez is a common name among the migrant workers in the area. The name Gonzo could refer to one of them." Bailey looked at Alex and shrugged her shoulders.

"Good to know," Elizabeth said. "Anything else you need to update us on?"

"Anyone have anything yet on why the grandpa was so rich while the son was so poor?" Alex asked.

"Not yet," Sydney replied. "I'm still checking into that and the shrimping and sugar cane industries."

"And I'm still researching to see if there were any other grandchildren and if Gonzo's father was living when his father dried," Kate added.

"Great." Alex gave Bailey a thumbs-up.

"I think that covers it," Bailey said. "Did we forget anything, Alex?"

"Not that I can think of."

"What about Yeller, Dude, and Rude? Have you seen any more of them?" McKenzie asked.

"No, not since Yeller fell out of the tree outside our window." Alex shivered thinking about it. "But we plan to walk down that way later today. We may see them then."

"How about if I say a little prayer for all of us before we hang up?" Elizabeth asked.

"Sure!" Bailey said. The line grew quiet.

"Dear God, we know You hear us and care about us," Elizabeth began. "Help us solve this mystery about Marshall Gonzalez. Most of all, keep us all safe as we work on it, especially Bailey and Alex. Give us wisdom and insight and help us to honor You in everything we do. Be with Gonzo, wherever he is, and keep him safe, too. In Jesus' name, amen."

"Amen!" the other five girls said in unison.

Bailey sighed. "I feel better already."

"Keep us posted on what you find out," Alex said to the girls. "We're keeping a file here of all the details so we can keep track of them."

"Will do," Kate said.

"I think that covers it then." Bailey looked in Alex's direction and saw her nod. "We'll call you with updates." Bailey flipped her phone closed.

"Let's take that walk down toward Yeller's place." Alex got up from the bed.

"We need to take a snack for Fang so he doesn't eat us alive," Bailey said, remembering the growling dog that chased them. She stuffed some cheese crackers in one of her jeans pockets and her inhaler and lip balm in the other. "I think we're ready."

"Have your camera, just in case?"

"Check." Bailey patted her wristwatch.

"I don't know why, but I feel nervous." Alex bit her cuticle.

"I know what you mean. I have a whole flock of butterflies racing around in my stomach." Bailey rubbed her tummy. "We're probably just excited. After all, we're just going for a walk, right?"

CHAPTER
8
★ ★ ★ ★

The Man Named Gonzo

Bailey and Alex crossed the front yard and ambled down the country road that ran alongside the Curly Q. Shy scampered to catch up with them then ran around them in circles to herd them along.

"Hi, girl," Alex said, rubbing the dog. A gentle breeze blew their hair back as they walked.

"Uh-oh." Bailey grimaced. "We forgot to tell anyone we were going for a walk."

"We'll probably be back before the guys are done shearing anyway, and your Aunt Darcy won't be home from work until after five."

"You're right. It's only one thirty now." Bailey reached for her lip balm. "We have plenty of time."

The girls walked a few paces in silence.

"Let's see if there's a sign by the creek up ahead that tells its history," Alex said. "Since Woolly Creek's name used to be Brindle Creek, maybe we'll learn something that gives us a clue to the 'Brindle Branch' message."

"I don't remember seeing one before, but we can check." Shy ran on ahead of the girls and disappeared in the brush along the side of the road.

When they reached the creek, they spotted Shy at the edge of the water, helping herself to a drink.

Alex looked around for a sign. "Looks like you were right. No sign with Woolly Creek's history on it."

"We'll just have to keep our eyes and ears open to find out about Brindle Branch." Bailey swatted a fly away. "Let's walk along the creek. I think it's low enough that Yeller, Dude, and Rude won't see us too easily when we pass their property."

The girls climbed down to where Shy was lapping water and began their creek walk.

"Do you really think their house is the same as Hazelwood Sheep Farms?" Alex asked.

Bailey shrugged. "It sure sounds like the same place Sydney's research turned up."

"Seems weird that it would be so run-down if they were still auctioning sheep just last spring."

Bailey could almost see the wheels turning in her friend's mind.

"Didn't you say Gonzo was getting into sheep farming before he disappeared?" Alex asked.

"Yeah."

"If he lived around here, then there should be some sign of his sheep farm, don't you think?"

"After seven years? I doubt it," Bailey said.

"Yeah, maybe that would be too long." Disappointment filled Alex's voice.

"We can still look for clues to his farm while we investigate Hazelwood Sheep Farms. After all, isn't that the real reason for this walk?"

"I guess," Alex said. "But that means going on Yeller, Dude, and Rude's property. Could be dangerous."

"Well, how else are we going to find out what we need to know?"

"I don't know, but going over there gives me the creeps." Alex shivered.

"What could happen?" Bailey asked.

"For starters, we could be eaten alive by Fang!"

"I brought snacks for him, remember?" Bailey patted her pocket. "Before you know it, we'll be Fang's best friends, and he'll wag his tail every time he sees us."

"I don't know. . ." Alex hesitated. "What if they see us?"

"Maybe we'll get a chance to talk to them. They may hold the answer to this mystery, you know."

"Maybe you're right." Alex looked around nervously.

"We'll let Shy lead the way. Dogs can detect danger before humans. But first we need to get to the other side of the creek."

Alex followed Bailey a short distance to a narrow part of the creek. Stones formed natural steps across the shallow water, and Bailey hopped effortlessly from one to the next. Safely on the other side, she turned around and saw Alex only halfway across. Her arms were stretched out to her sides for balance. She teetered on one stone, and then stepped gingerly to the next.

"Don't worry, they're not slippery!" Bailey yelled above the sound of the creek and the sheep bleating from her uncle's pasture.

Shy waded through the water, circling Alex, trying to herd her along like a stray lamb, but Alex continued on at her own cautious pace. Finally, she drew close enough for Bailey to reach out and take her hand. Alex grabbed it like a lifeline, and Bailey pulled her friend onto the bank.

"You did it!" Bailey hugged Alex.

Shy jumped out of the creek and shook her wet fur, spraying the girls like a sprinkler.

"Shy!" Bailey yelled, wiping off her arms. She looked at Alex and laughed. A drop of water hung from the tip of her friend's nose, and her green cotton T-shirt and gray gym shorts were speckled with wet spots. Tiny rivulets ran down her bare legs.

Alex exploded in laughter. "That dog!"

"Come on," Bailey said, wiping water from her face with her shirt. "Now that we look so nice, let's go visit the neighbors."

Alex giggled. "I needed a good laugh to get over my nerves. I think I'm ready now."

"Lead the way, Shy." Bailey followed the wet dog along the creek bank. "Remember, keep your eyes open for any signs of Gonzo's sheep or Hazelwood Sheep Farms."

"Right," Alex answered. "If we spread out a bit, we can cover more territory." Alex stayed close to the water while Bailey went further ashore. Shy jogged between the two.

The trio marched along, sometimes heads down looking for clues, and other times heads up, keeping nervous watch for any sign of Yeller, Dude, and Rude.

"Look at this!" Bailey stopped and stared at a dry, brown clump.

Alex stepped over rocks at the creek's edge and hurried to Bailey. "What is it?"

"Looks like dry sheep droppings," Bailey said kneeling down.

"Terrific!" Alex said, half smiling. "It can't be from Gonzo's farm, or it would have disintegrated into the soil by now."

"No, but it could be from Hazelwood sheep." Bailey stood and kicked the dry clump with the toe of her tennis shoe. "Let's keep looking."

Alex returned to her place by the water's edge, and they continued their search. Shy sniffed the ground.

"Hey, check this out!" Alex yelled a short time later.

Bailey saw Alex squatting by the water. As she came closer, Alex reached into the creek. "What's up?" Bailey asked her.

"I found something." Alex pulled a small yellow plastic tag with a number on it out of the water. The five-sided tag came to a rounded off point like a triangle at the top, but the sides and bottom were squared, making the whole thing the shape of a tiny house.

"Looks like an ear tag from a sheep." Bailey held out her hand, and Alex dropped the tag into it. "There's a number on both sides. The tags are used for identification, but I don't know how to read them or what they mean."

"Maybe Brian knows!" Alex's hopeful eyes danced.

"We'll ask him when we get home." Bailey handed the tag back to Alex, who slid it into her shirt pocket. "Wow! We're almost past Yeller's house already."

"And no sign of Fang, thank goodness!" Alex added.

"Let's keep looking." Alex and Bailey split up again. Suddenly Shy took off ahead of them.

She's sure in a hurry. Bailey kept walking, eyes to the ground. Her head shot up when she heard Shy bark, though she couldn't see the Australian shepherd.

"I think Shy's found something!" Bailey yelled. She and Alex ran toward the sound, staying low toward the creek until they were safely past Yeller's backyard. They spied Shy by a fenced sheep pasture, barking. The sheep baaed and scattered in confused dismay at this unfamiliar dog making so much noise.

"Sheep!" Bailey shouted at Alex. They reached Shy, out of breath. The dog settled down as soon as the girls reached her side.

"I wonder who they belong to." Alex covered her nose at the foul smell.

"I don't know, but they look—and smell—awful!" Bailey wrinkled her nose and frowned. "Uncle Nathan would have a fit if his flock looked like this." Bailey went closer to inspect the sickly sheep. "Look at this poor, skinny ewe. She has a runny nose, her hooves need trimming, and she has sores on her head. These sheep are half starved. Some of them can barely walk! I bet they have parasites, too. Uncle Nathan is always watching his flock for signs of them because they're so common with sheep."

Alex nodded her head. "Poor things."

"Hey! What are you doing?" a gruff voice yelled. A man ran toward Bailey and Alex, a fist raised in the air. Shy barked again.

"We're just out for a walk and stopped to see the sheep," Bailey answered innocently, but the man appeared not to hear her. He stomped closer, his arms swinging madly with each step.

"Bailey!" Alex said. "That's Dude!"

"Or Rude," Bailey added, "since we don't know which is which."

"We'd better go!" Alex grabbed Bailey's hand.

"No! Wait!" Bailey pulled her hand away. "This could be our chance to ask a few questions," she whispered.

"You're on private property!" the wiry man growled. He wore a dirty white T-shirt and grimy jeans. His greasy brown hair looked like he'd just crawled out of bed.

"We're sorry," Alex said. "We didn't know."

"Are these your sheep?" Bailey asked.

"Yeah, they're mine. What of it?" the man answered, his voice low and raspy. The deep lines in his weathered face contorted in anger.

"How long have you been sheep farming?" Bailey tried to sound like a friendly neighbor.

"None of your business."

"I'm Bailey, and this is my friend, Alex." Bailey stuck out her hand for the man to shake. She hoped he didn't notice its tremble. "We're here visiting my uncle. We leave on Saturday."

The man's shoulders relaxed with that bit of news, and he hesitantly shook Bailey's hand. He stared at them, his face clouded with suspicion.

Behind her smile, Bailey gritted her teeth, resisting the urge to wipe her hand on her jeans after shaking the man's dirt-encrusted hand.

"What's your name?" Alex asked, her face a mask of sweet innocence.

Bailey could tell her friend had caught on to her friendly, naive, chatty-girls-asking-questions strategy.

The man didn't respond, and Bailey cringed at his stony glare.

Bailey shrugged, maintaining the naive, chatty-girls plan. "Ever hear of someone named Gonzo?"

The man's small, close-set blue eyes widened slightly, and he squared his shoulders. "Gonzo? That's *my* name!"

Bailey stood up straight. "*You're* Gonzo?"

Shy took a tentative step or two and growled low and throaty.

Alex's mouth hung open. "B–but. . .you're supposed to be dead!"

"Huh?" Gonzo frowned.

Grrrowuf! Just then Fang charged across the yard at

them in a snarling mass of teeth and fur. Shy barked back just as fiercely and flew toward the muscular dog.

"Shy! No!" Bailey screamed. She tore after the dog toward the weed-ridden yard of the neglected house.

Alex followed on Bailey's heels. The girls saw Yeller standing by the barn trying to call off the dog. A third man, either Dude or Rude, pulled Yeller out of sight.

"I. . .can't. . .breathe," Bailey gasped, reaching into her pocket for her inhaler. She searched the wrong pocket and found the snack she brought for Fang. Between wheezes, she ripped open the package, and tossed it at him. Then she stuck her hand in the other pocket and grasped her inhaler. Dropping to the ground, she quickly uncapped it, put it in her mouth, and squeezed.

"Keep. . .running toward. . .home!" she told Alex. "Shy will. . .follow you. She's. . .just trying. . .to protect us." Bailey glanced at the pasture where the sick sheep were. Her skin crawled when she spotted Gonzo leaning against the fence.

"I'm not leaving you here!" Alex yelled.

"Go!" Bailey commanded. "I'll be. . .behind you." Her mouth was dry and her palms sweaty as she struggled to stand.

Alex helped her up and then did as she was told. Bailey trailed her as closely as she was able. She heard the snarling and growling of the dogs fighting. The cheese crackers she tossed to Fang apparently hadn't slowed him down. Shy yelped. Moments later the dog limped beside the girls.

"And *stay* away!" Bailey heard one of the men yell. Then

he roared with laughter.

"Don't look back," Alex said. As they neared the road, they slowed to a walk. "Are you okay?"

Bailey nodded, still gasping for breath.

"Good thing you had your inhaler along this time."

"Yeah." Bailey crouched down to look at Shy. "You okay, girl?"

The dog nuzzled Bailey's face and licked her.

Bailey wrapped her arms around Shy's neck, breathing deeply to slow her pulse. "That awful dog bit the back of your neck," she said moving Shy's fur aside. "And look at your leg. You got some pretty nasty cuts there. Come on. Let's go see Uncle Nathan."

"How will we explain this?" Alex asked.

"What's to explain?" Bailey replied. "We went for a walk by the creek and a mean dog attacked Shy."

"That's *it*?"

"What more do we need to say?" Bailey asked with her eyebrows raised.

"What about the men? What about Gonzo?"

"What about them?"

"Don't you think we should tell your uncle what happened?" Alex nearly yelled.

"Nothing happened!" Bailey yelled back. "The guy said his name was Gonzo. The dog got loose, and we ran. End of story."

"He warned us not to come back." Alex looked sideways at her friend.

"He didn't warn us," Bailey said. "He just said to stay away."

"Same thing."

"Look. We're closer now than we've ever been to solving this mystery. Please," Bailey pleaded, "let's not mess it up now."

Alex sighed and rolled her eyes. "Oh, all right," she mumbled. "But if anything else happens, we have to tell."

"Deal." Bailey hugged Alex. "Friends?"

Alex laughed. "Of course. Always."

"We need to ask Brian about this sheep tag." Alex patted her shirt pocket. "Oh no, Bailey! It's gone!"

The Old Wooden Sign

"How could it be gone?" Bailey asked. "You put it in your pocket just awhile ago."

"It must have bounced out when we were running." Alex turned, scanning the yard of dirt and tall weeds they had just crossed.

"I bet we could find it if we retraced our steps," Bailey said.

"I'm not going back there!" Alex's jaw clenched. "I just got my heart rate back to normal. Besides, we need to get Shy home."

Looking one last time at the run-down house, Bailey scratched Shy behind the ears. "I guess you're right. Come on, girl. Let's go."

The girls hurried back to the house, Shy limping along beside them.

"Uncle Nathan!" Bailey called as they approached the barn, but the shears drowned out her voice. Her uncle turned them off when he spotted them.

"What are you two up to?" he asked.

"Uncle Nathan, Shy's been hurt," Bailey told him.

Uncle Nathan hurried to them and bent to inspect

his sheepdog. Bailey knew Shy was not only a part of the family, but she played an important role in his sheep business. He tenderly lifted the injured leg. "She may need stitches. I'd better get her to Doc Maddox."

"She has a cut on her neck, too." Bailey spread Shy's fur to show him.

"That one doesn't look quite as bad." Uncle Nathan picked up Shy like Bailey had often seen him pick up lambs and headed toward his truck. "Tell Brian we're leaving while I load her into the truck."

Bailey did as she was told and was back moments later.

"What happened to her?" Uncle Nathan asked as Bailey climbed into the truck.

"We were taking a walk down by the creek," Alex began.

"And a big, mean dog charged out from that old house across the creek," Bailey finished.

"We think Shy tried to protect us by going after the dog." Alex frowned.

"Shy fought that dog like mad until we were safely past." Bailey sighed sadly. "Then she caught up with us and we came home."

"Were you on our side of the creek?"

Bailey glanced at Alex. "No, we had crossed the creek."

Uncle Nathan looked at Bailey in his rearview mirror. "Why'd you do that?"

Bailey licked her lips. "I. . .I don't know. We found a safe place to cross with stepping-stones and everything. The water wasn't deep."

"The water's never deep," her uncle replied sternly. "But the other side of the creek is someone else's property. You shouldn't go there without permission."

Bailey grew quiet for a moment. "Uncle Nathan, we found out they're keeping sheep over there and aren't taking care of them," she said, not sure if she should tell him. "You should see them. They're skin and bones, their noses are runny, their hooves need trimming. It'd make you sick!" Her voice rose passionately.

Uncle Nathan's eyes darted to his mirror. "Did you see the owners?" he asked.

Bailey and Alex exchanged looks. *The truth.* Bailey knew what was right, and she had to do it. "Yeah, we met one of the owners." Her voice sounded reluctant.

"Bailey. . .what are you not telling me?" Uncle Nathan pressed.

"He said his name was Gonzo. He was filthy, and he didn't even try to help Shy or us when his dog chased us!" Her words spilled out like water over a cliff. Unexpected tears sprang to Bailey's eyes. She wasn't sure if they were from having to admit what they'd done or from the fear she felt as Shy was being attacked.

"We heard him—or one of the other men—laugh as we ran away," Alex added.

"Other men? What other men?" Uncle Nathan asked.

"We saw one man by the barn, and he tried to call off the dog," Bailey explained. "But another man jerked him back into the barn."

Her uncle's temples moved as he ground his teeth. A blue vein bulged on his forehead, but he said nothing. Finally, he blew air from his mouth, like steam being released from a pressurized pot.

"I will have a word with our neighbor," he said in carefully measured words. "That will *never* happen again. These men sound cruel, and I don't want you near them. Stay off their property. You hear?"

"Yes, sir," Bailey said softly.

"We're sorry about all this," Alex said, remorse filling her voice.

"I know you are. It's okay. At least you weren't hurt."

"But Shy was," Bailey said, her voice trembling. She brushed away hot tears.

"Shy'll be fine. Doc Maddox will stitch her, and she'll be good as new in a few days," Uncle Nathan reassured her. "She's used to having to protect the sheep. She's fought off worse than that dog before."

They arrived at the vet's office, and Uncle Nathan carried Shy in.

Bailey's spirits rose at the good report Doc Maddox gave after examining the sheepdog. "She'll be chasing sheep again in no time!"

Turned out Uncle Nathan was right. Doc Maddox sewed Shy up in minutes, and they headed back home.

"Hey, look at that." Uncle Nathan pointed out his window. "A flea market. Should we stop?"

"Yeah!" Bailey yelled.

They pulled into the parking lot, rolled the windows down a little for Shy, and got out. "I'm going to look at the tool booth," Uncle Nathan said.

"Ugh, tools," Bailey teased her uncle. "Can we look around at other stuff? We have our cell phones, so you can call us when you're ready to go."

"You don't want to look at tools with me?" Uncle Nathan grinned and winked. "I guess you can look at something else."

"Thanks! See ya!" Bailey and Alex took off.

The girls fingered hair accessories, stuffed animals, and wind chimes. They tried on hats and laughed at their reflections in the mirror.

"Look at this booth," Alex said. "Everything is carved out of wood."

"Cool!" Bailey picked up a small wooden sign with her name carved in it, then set it back down and continued browsing. "Alex, look!" Her eyes were fixed on a rough sign carved out of old barn wood hanging with other used items.

"BRINDLE BRANCH FARM!" Alex's mouth fell open as soon as she read the words.

"May I help you?" An older man, with a face that looked like it, too, had been hewn from old wood, stood beside them.

"Yes," Alex replied. "We were wondering about that Brindle Branch sign."

"Oh yes, she's a beauty, isn't she?" the man said.

"Do you know anything about its history?" Bailey

pointed her watch at the sign and snapped a picture when the man turned his back.

"We got that sign in several weeks ago from a sheep farmer. Said it used to be the name of his property, and the sign hung over the front door of his farmhouse."

"Used to be the name?" Alex asked. "Did he say what the farm's called now?"

"No. Sorry, he didn't."

"What did the man look like?" Bailey asked.

"What did he look like?" The man chuckled softly. "I'm afraid I don't remember." He thought a moment. "Kinda dark, maybe, sort of tall." He waved his hand in dismay. "Aw, I don't know. I get too many people in here to remember what one man looks like."

"Do you know where this Brindle Branch Farm was located?" Alex twisted a curl around her finger.

"Can't say I do. Must not be too far though, or this fellow probably wouldn't have brought the sign here, I suppose."

"How much does it cost?" Bailey felt for her wallet.

"Twenty dollars."

Bailey looked at Alex. "We'll think about it. Thanks for the information."

"My pleasure." The man turned to help another customer.

"I only have ten dollars with me," Bailey told Alex.

"Let me see how much I have." Alex did a quick count. "Eight dollars and seventy-eight cents."

"Not enough to buy that sign." Bailey sighed.

"Unless he'll let us have it for less." Alex smiled. "They often do that at flea markets!"

"Good idea!" Bailey said. "You want to ask him?"

Alex went up to the old gentleman and cleared her throat. "Excuse me, sir."

"Yes, how can I help you?"

"That Brindle Branch sign. Would you take fifteen dollars for it?"

The man's forehead wrinkled. "Fifteen? Hmm. I don't know. . . ."

"Please, sir," Bailey begged. "It's practically all the money we have with us."

The man eyed them carefully and then melted like butter on a hot biscuit. "Oh, I guess fifteen would be all right. No one else has even looked at it in the time we've had it." His eyes sparkled at the girls as he lifted the sign off its hook and wrapped it in brown paper.

"That'll be sixteen dollars and twenty cents with tax."

"Great!" Bailey smiled at the man and handed him the cash. "You don't know how much this means to us!"

"I don't know why young gals like you would want an old beat-up sign like that, but I'm glad you like it."

The girls walked down the row of booths. "We still have enough money left over to buy a treat from the candy booth." Bailey's mouth watered at the idea.

The girls each chose a treat—Skittles for Bailey and a granola bar for Alex.

Bailey's phone vibrated in her pocket. "Hello?"

"I'm done at the tool booth. Are you girls ready to go?" Uncle Nathan asked.

"Yep. We bought a cool sign and a treat, so we're all ready."

"I'll meet you at the entrance."

"Okay. See you in a minute." Bailey shoved her phone into her pocket.

"We're supposed to meet Uncle Nathan at the entrance."

Alex nodded. "Hey, Bailey?"

"Yeah?"

"I'm sorry I was afraid to go retrace our steps to look for the ear tag."

"No biggie. Besides, now we have this sign to investigate."

"Maybe tomorrow I'll feel braver," Alex offered.

"Do you remember anything about the ear tag?"

"It was yellow and shaped like a tiny house. And it was made of plastic."

"Any idea what the numbers on it were?" Bailey pressed.

"Not for sure." Alex paused. "I think one side might have said forty-six. Or maybe it was sixty-four."

"Great!" Bailey squealed. "I think the other side said five-one-two-nine! At least I'm *pretty* sure those were the numbers. I'm just not positive of their order."

"Now if we can get Brian to tell us what the numbers mean, we're all set." Alex's grin stretched as wide as a slice of watermelon. "Maybe we won't need to look for the tag after all!"

They saw Uncle Nathan waiting. He spotted their bag right away. "Let's see this cool sign you found," he said.

Bailey carefully pulled it from the bag and unwrapped it.

"BRINDLE BRANCH FARM," Uncle Nathan read. "Hmm. That sounds familiar."

"It does?" Alex's eyes flew open.

"Do you know where it is?" Bailey asked.

"Can't say that I do, but I've heard of it."

"The sign looks old, don't you think?"

Running a calloused hand over it, her uncle said, "Looks old, all right." He looked at the girls and smiled. "You *did* find a pretty cool sign. It has a lot of character!"

"We're going to research its history and see what we can find out." Bailey rewrapped it in the brown paper before returning it to its bag.

"That should be interesting," Uncle Nathan said. "I'd be curious to know what you find out."

"We'll let you know," Alex said.

Uncle Nathan unlocked the truck, and Shy sat up, yawned, and looked around.

"Looks like someone's been taking a nap," Uncle Nathan said. "Must be tuckered out from such an adventurous afternoon."

When Shy saw them, she stood up on the backseat, her tail wagging like it was attached to a spring. Her mouth parted in a dog smile, her tongue dangling out the side.

Bailey opened the door. "Hi, girl!" She climbed in and was greeted with a face full of wet kisses. "Are you feeling better?"

"Sure looks like it!" Alex said, laughing.

"Uncle Nathan, did you know that Woolly Creek behind your house used to be called Brindle Creek?" Bailey asked.

"Brindle Creek? No, I didn't." Uncle Nathan made a funny face. "How'd you know that?"

"We saw it at the Historical Society a couple days ago." Bailey buckled her seat belt.

"Well, I'll be!"

"So maybe Brindle Branch Farm is along that creek somewhere," Alex said.

"Could be," Uncle Nathan said. "Sounds like you're off to a good start already with researching that sign you bought. But remember, no more going onto someone else's property without permission. You could have been hurt today."

"We won't, Uncle Nathan," Bailey assured him.

Minutes later, the truck pulled into the driveway of Uncle Nathan's home. The girls jumped out and headed toward the house.

"I'll see you gals at supper. I have some shearing to finish." Uncle Nathan waved them off and went back to join Brian in the barn.

In their bedroom, Alex sat on the floor, her back against the foot of the bed. She opened the laptop and checked her e-mail.

"Anything interesting?" Bailey asked.

"Not much. My mom sent me a note." Alexis smiled. "She misses me."

"She won't have to miss you much longer," Bailey said. "We'll be home soon."

"I know. I can't believe how fast this week is going."

"Only two more days to solve this mystery. What do you think we should do next?"

Alex cocked her head. "I'm guessing Brindle Branch Farm must be along Brindle Creek, which is now called Woolly Creek."

"Yeah."

"So tomorrow we should take another walk along the creek—making sure we stay on our own side—to see if we can figure out which place is Brindle Branch."

Bailey perked up. "Maybe we could even talk to some of the neighbors. They may know something."

"Great idea!"

"One way or another, we'll solve this mystery of Marshall Gonzalez and Brindle Branch and the marked sheep," Bailey said.

There was a knock on the girls' door.

"Come in!" Bailey called.

Brian stuck his head in the door. "Dad let me off early since there were only a few sheep left when he got back. I heard *you* had an exciting day!"

"Boy, did we ever!" Bailey answered. "Come on in."

Brian plunked down in the pink beanbag. Bailey and Alex retold the events of the day.

"Wow," he finally said. "I'm glad you guys are okay. Wish I'd been along. I'd have made those guys sorry for messing with you." He winked at Alex.

Alex turned beet red and looked down at her feet. A hint of a smile played on her lips.

Puffing out her chest and holding her head up high, Bailey bragged, "We handled it very well ourselves, thank you."

"Oh! We have something to ask you," Alex said, her color returning to normal.

"Oh yeah! I almost forgot," Bailey added. "Do you know anything about ear tags?"

"Sure. What about them?" Brian sat up straighter.

"What do the numbers mean?" Bailey asked.

"Each farm is given an identification number by the Department of Agriculture. They require that every sheep be given a premise identification ear tag before leaving the farm where it was born. They call it their premise ID. That number goes on one side of the tag." Brian looked from girl to girl. "Care to guess what the number on the other side of the tag is?"

"The sheep's number!" Alex yelled.

Brian pointed at her. "You got it!" He leaned over to Bailey and muttered loud enough for Alex to hear, "I knew she was a smart one."

Bailey laughed.

"Each sheep is given a number when it's purchased," Brian explained. "Often the first number shows the animal's birth year, and the rest of the number is sequential. That number goes on the other side of the tag."

"Do the colors of the tags mean anything?" Alex asked.

"They can, but that's up to the farmer. He may color code them according to age, breed types, or owners."

"So a yellow tag may mean something different depending on the farm?" Bailey asked.

"Exactly. Why do you ask?"

"I found an ear tag in the creek before we were charged by Fang."

"Well, let's see it! Maybe I can tell you whose it is!" Brian said, stretching out his hand.

"I can't. It fell out of my pocket when we were running away from the dog." Alex's voice sounded disappointed.

"No way!" Brian said, a smile tugging the corners of his mouth.

Bailey nodded.

"But we think we remember the numbers," Alex said, her voice hopeful. "I think one side was forty-six—or sixty-four."

"And the other side said five-one-two-nine, but not necessarily in that order," Bailey added.

"I think I can help you," Brian said, jumping up from the beanbag. "I'll be right back."

CHAPTER 10

The List of Clues

Brian rushed out the door before Bailey and Alex could speak.

The girls looked at each other. Bailey shrugged and said, "I guess he has an idea."

Alex laughed. "Obviously!"

Brian flew back in minutes later, Uncle Nathan's ledger tucked under his arm. He closed the door behind him and flopped onto the beanbag. "I remember seeing a chart of farms and their IDs listed in here." Brian flipped through the pages. "Ah! Here it is."

He ran his finger down a column, all the while mumbling, "Forty-six. . .forty-six." His finger stopped on the second page, and he looked up with a grin.

"Well, did you find it?" Bailey asked.

"Yep, I've got it right here." His fingers tapped the open page.

"So which farm is it?" Alex urged. She craned her neck, trying to get a look at the book.

"What'll you give me for telling you?" Brian teased.

"I'll give you another day to live! Now tell us which farm it is!" Bailey snapped.

Brian laughed. "You're so fun to mess with. All right. I'll tell you. It's Hazelwood Farm."

"That's what we figured." Alex slumped against the foot of the bed. "We're pretty sure that's the name of the farm on the other side of the creek where those terrible men live."

"Then why were you so cranked up to find out?"

"We just wanted to be sure, that's all." Bailey sighed.

"Anything else you want to know before I put the book back?"

"Does it say anything else about how they identify their sheep?" Alex asked.

"What do you mean?" Brian's forehead wrinkled.

"Like, do they only use ear tags, or do they use other things?"

"Hmm. I'll look." Brian thumbed through a few pages and then stopped. "It says they sometimes use paint sticks to temporarily mark sheep before selling them."

"Paint sticks? That's it!" Bailey jumped up from the bed.

"That's what?" Brian asked.

"I bet that's what the words on the lambs were written with!" Bailey reached down and gave Alex's raised hand a high five.

"You're probably right." Brian nodded. "Permanent markers probably wouldn't be good for the sheep."

"But paint sticks wouldn't hurt them?" Alex asked.

"No. They're specially made to be nontoxic."

"How long does it last?" Bailey wondered.

"Usually several months," Brian replied.

"Over six months?" Bailey pressed, knowing the sheep were only sheared that often.

"Yeah. Often a farmer will paint-brand their ewes when they're pregnant and then give the same number to their babies once they're born and until they're given their own number. It makes it easier to match the mothers and babies."

"Why didn't you tell us about paint-branding before?" Bailey asked. "We were trying to sniff those marked sheep to see if they smelled like permanent marker!"

Brian laughed. "You *would* do something crazy like that." He shrugged. "I don't know. I guess I just didn't think about it."

"That brings us one step closer to solving this mystery," Alex said.

"Speaking of clues to the mystery," Bailey said, "do you want to see the sign we got at the flea market today?"

"Sure," Brian said.

Bailey unwrapped it and showed the sign to her cousin.

"Sweet!" Brian took the sign in his hands. He studied the words carved into the front and then turned it over. "Hey, look at this. The carver's initials."

"Huh?" Bailey was at Brian's side in an instant. Alex flanked his other side.

"See? M. G." Brian pointed at small letters in the lower left corner.

"Marshall Gonzalez!" Bailey whooped.

"Could be," Alex agreed.

"Why would you automatically think it was Marshall Gonzalez?" Brian looked wary. "Could be Matthew Gardner or Mike Green."

"I guess you're right," Alex conceded. "We just have Marshall on the brain."

"We have to solve this mystery in two days, so we need to stay focused," Bailey reminded her cousin.

Brian nodded. "Well, you're certainly doing that."

"We need to research Brindle Branch Farm," Bailey said.

"I'll Google it." Alex set her computer in her lap.

"It's as good a place to start as any." Bailey stretched out on her stomach, her head at the foot of the bed, to look over Alex's shoulder.

Five entries came up. Alex clicked on the first one. Up popped an article about adopting brindle greyhound dogs. She quickly clicked out and went to the next one. *Brindle Branch Farm, located in Peoria, Illinois. . .*

"Alex! That's it!" Bailey squealed.

"Read it out loud," Brian said from the pink beanbag.

Alex cleared her throat. "Brindle Branch Farm, located in Peoria, Illinois, is a historic sheep farm once known for its high-quality wool production. It stopped wool operation in 2000, but its old house and farm buildings still stand. In 2002 the farm's name was changed to Hazelwood Sheep Farms."

"So Brindle Branch Farm is Hazelwood Sheep Farms, just as we suspected!" Bailey gave a victorious fist pump.

"Okay. Let's review what we know so far. Maybe it will help us connect the dots." Alex pulled out her notebook that listed the facts and clues they had accumulated. "First, Marshall Gonzalez disappeared seven years ago, and his relatives want him declared legally dead so they can claim his fortune."

"Two," Bailey piped in, reading over Alex's shoulder from the bed, "Marshall was a recluse. He didn't have many friends or close relatives."

"Three," Alex resumed, "investigators never found a body, so Marshall could be alive. Four, he lived around here somewhere and started sheep farming before his disappearance."

"Correction." Bailey cleared her throat. "Uncle Nathan said he *supposedly* mentioned going into sheep farming and even attended a sheep expo, but we don't know for sure if he started up a sheep farm."

"Point taken." Alex erased part of point four and wrote in the correction.

Bailey continued reading aloud. "Five, Marshall shut down his Peoria house and released all workers except for a caretaker. Six, three men and a mean dog live in that ramshackle house across the creek. We call them Yeller, Dude, Rude, and Fang. Dude and Rude try to keep Yeller from being seen or heard."

"Seven," Alex read on, "Yeller tried to get our attention. He was even ready to climb the tree outside our window at night."

"What?" Brian bolted upright, his eyes flashing.

Alex frowned at Bailey. "Oops."

"He climbed the tree outside your bedroom window?" Brian pressed.

Bailey's head drooped. "Only once. He fell out and limped away."

"Good! Maybe that will teach him not to slink around girls' bedroom windows! Why didn't you tell me or Dad?"

"Because we were afraid you'd make us stop investigating!" Bailey finally met Brian's eyes.

"You got that right! This could be some weirdo who could hurt you!" Brian stood and paced the room like a caged tiger.

"But he isn't!" Bailey wailed. "He just wants to tell us something. Something important!"

"How do you know?"

"Because the first time we saw him he waved at us and yelled. He was trying to get our attention."

"Yeah, then the other two hauled him back to the house." Alex nodded.

"And these are the same guys whose dog attacked Shy, and they didn't help you? They sound like real charmers to me." Brian rolled his eyes.

"Yeller tried to help, but the other guy wouldn't let him," Bailey said.

"It's true," Alex added. "The other guy pulled him into the barn."

Brian raked his hand through his dark curls. "We need to tell my dad."

"Brian, it's history! Over!" Bailey stood and planted

herself in his face, her hands on her hips.

"You don't know that." Brian took a deep breath and let it out slowly. "He could come back tonight for all you know."

"But I honestly don't think he's trying to hurt us. He would have already come back and tried. After all, that happened on Monday, and it's Friday now. He just wants to tell us something." Bailey sat back down.

Brian looked at Alex. "Do you agree?"

Alex nodded. "I thought we should tell at first. But now I don't think Yeller would hurt us. Like Bailey said, he's had all week to try again. The other guys might be dangerous, but not Yeller."

"I think he needs help," Bailey said.

Brian kept pacing, his eyebrows forming a *V*. Bailey watched him until he stopped in front of them.

"I'll make you a deal," he said. "You promise to call me on my cell phone the second anything *potentially* happens with these guys. Even if they look at you cross-eyed! And I won't tell Dad."

Alex quietly nodded. Bailey sighed with relief. "I promise, Brian." She wrapped her arms around his waist, laying her head on his chest. "Thanks."

Brian patted Bailey on the back. "Now, where were you on that list of clues?" he said.

Alex laughed. "Let's see, I think we were on number eight." She looked to the notebook. "Yes. Eight. We have three messages written on lambs. Together they read, 'Help Gonzo held captive Brindle Branch.' Number nine, Kate dug up that Gonzalez was from Sinoloa, Mexico. He's the son of a poor shrimp fisherman, but his grandpa was a rich sugar cane farmer. Grandpa left Gonzalez his fortune when he died. So jealousy could be a motive for his relatives wanting him declared dead."

"Number ten," Bailey jumped in. "Woolly Creek behind the Curly Q used to be called Brindle Creek. The name was changed twenty years ago."

"Eleven," Alex said. "Curly Q sheep were bought at auctions from three farms: Hazelwood Sheep Farms, Hollyhock Acres, and Whitestone Ranch. Hazelwood is the closest, just across the creek. Twelve, the kidnapping may have been done by someone Gonzalez knew. The kidnapper would have to care for Gonzo's sheep, and they only follow their own shepherd's voice. Thirteen, I found an ear tag with the number forty-six on one side and five-one-two-nine on the other."

"Fourteen," Bailey said. "There are sick sheep living in the pasture behind the house. They're not being cared for properly."

"Fifteen," Alex stated. "The man at the sheep pasture said his name is Gonzo, but he doesn't look like the newspaper photo of Marshall Gonzalez. He's taller and thinner."

"And dirtier!" Bailey added with a laugh. "Sixteen. Brindle Branch Farm was a sheep farm. The sign that bears its name was carved by someone with the initials M. G."

"Seventeen," Alex said. "Brindle Branch Farm was probably located on Brindle Creek, which is now Woolly Creek."

"Last but not least, number forty-six from the ear tag Alex found belongs to Hazelwood Sheep Farms, which used to be called Brindle Branch Farm. They probably use paint sticks to temporarily brand their sheep when new babies are born.

"And," Bailey added, "those paint sticks might be what the messages on the lambs were written with."

"Wow." Brian shook his head appreciatively. "You guys have dug up a lot of information in only a few days."

"We had to! We only have a few days to figure this whole thing out!"

"Wait a minute!" Alex's eyes blazed. "We missed an obvious step!"

Bailey's forehead creased. "We did? What?"

"The ear tags! We know Hazelwood Farms' ID is forty-six. Now we need to see if the lambs with the messages have the same ID!"

Bailey clapped her hands. "You're right! How could we have missed that?"

"Good thing we reviewed our notebook. It really did help us connect some ideas!"

"So what are we waiting for?" Brian asked. "Let's go check some ear tags."

All three were out the door in the shake of a lamb's tail. They ran into Aunt Darcy in the kitchen.

"Supper will be ready soon. Don't go too far."

"We won't," Brian answered. "We're just going out to see some of the lambs." He winked at the girls.

The three ran across the yard to the pasture, slowing as they approached so as not to scare the sheep. Shy limped along in the chase. Opening the gate, they pushed their way through the flock. Bow nuzzled their hands for some attention.

Bailey absently stroked the lamb's head. "I don't see them." Her head turned to look first one way, then another.

"Me neither," Brian said.

"They've got to be here somewhere," Alex encouraged. "We just need to keep looking."

They split up, and each took a section to search, but they couldn't find the marked sheep.

"Where could they be?" Bailey asked.

Brian looked stricken.

"Brian, what is it?" Bailey eyed her cousin.

"Sometimes Dad separates the animals that are going to be sold."

"Sold? He can't sell those lambs! It would be like selling Charlotte in *Charlotte's Web*!" Alex wailed.

"Yeah, they're communicating with us just like she did in her spiderweb," Bailey agreed.

"I remember hearing Dad say some men were coming this afternoon to look over some of our young sheep. Some of them might be the ones with the weird markings."

"Now we'll never find out which ranch the sheep came from!" Bailey felt like throwing herself on the ground. Disappointment curled through her like a giant wave from her stomach to her eyes, threatening tears. She took a deep breath and let it back out.

"I didn't say they'd been sold already, but he may have separated them from the others," Brian said gently.

"So where are they?" Bailey demanded.

"Could be a number of places—in a different pasture, in the barn, or maybe at another farm already."

"We've got to find them." Bailey looked around. "Which place should we check first?"

"The barn's the closest. Let's go there," Alex suggested.

Without a word, they worked back through the flock of milling sheep and out the gate to the barn. Shy trotted with them, happy and unconcerned. Bow baaed her dismay when they walked away. Bailey knew before they ever set foot in the barn that the lambs weren't there. It was too quiet. But the trio walked through the building checking each stall.

"Maybe they're just sleeping in a pen somewhere," Alex said hopefully.

"They're not here," Bailey said.

"Where do we look next, Brian?" Alex asked.

"The other pasture," Brian said. "But it's too far to go before supper."

"It'll be getting dark after that!" Bailey moaned.

"If they're in the far pasture, they'll still be there in the morning," Brian said matter-of-factly. "And if they're not, we probably won't find them anyway."

Bailey thought she might cry but bit her lip hard to hold back the tears. Their best clue. Gone!

The Lost Sheep

Bailey and Alex trudged back to the house while Brian secured the gates and made sure everything was closed tight.

"Those marked lambs were our best clue!" Frustration filled Bailey's voice.

"I know," Alex said. "It seems the odds are against us solving this mystery. But we have lots of other clues to work with. And we have pictures of the lambs' messages."

"Yeah, I guess. I just hope if the police get involved, they won't think we marked the sheep ourselves and then took pictures of our funny little joke. We have absolutely no proof."

"We didn't have proof even when we had the sheep."

They entered the kitchen, slamming the screen door behind them.

"Supper's ready as soon as you wash up," called Aunt Darcy, carrying a steaming casserole to the table and setting it on a trivet.

Bailey and Alex shared the bathroom sink as they washed their hands. "We'll have to ask Uncle Nathan about the lambs," Bailey suggested as she handed the towel to Alex.

"Just don't give away the investigation in the process," Alex warned.

Brian came in just as they returned to the kitchen. Bailey threw him a questioning look, but he shook his head on his way to wash up.

They all sat down, and Uncle Nathan asked God to bless the food.

"What is it?" Brian asked his mom as he lifted the casserole lid.

"Tuna casserole with peas." She uncovered a plate of warm, freshly made whole wheat bread and passed it to Bailey, along with the tub of butter.

"Mmm! This bread smells delicious!" Bailey gushed. She quickly spread a heap of butter on a slice and bit into it.

"How was your afternoon?" Uncle Nathan asked the girls. "I assume you didn't get chased by a dog."

Bailey laughed as she finished chewing the bread in her mouth. "No, nothing that exciting this afternoon."

"I can't believe all that happened only this morning." Alex shook her head, eyes wide. "Seems like days ago!"

"Time flies when you're having fun." Brian flashed a smile at Alex.

She quickly looked away, red creeping into her face.

"Uncle Nathan, did you move some lambs today?" Bailey tried to sound casual in her question, casting a glance at Alex.

"A few. They showed signs of getting hoof rot, so I had to quarantine them from the rest of the flock."

"Hoof rot?" Bailey passed the butter on to Alex.

"It's a fungal infection of the hoof that can lead to lameness if it isn't treated."

"How do they get it?" Alex asked.

"It usually happens when sheep spend long hours on wet grounds. That's why it's important to keep their bedding clean and dry."

"But we do that," Brian said and took a bite. After swallowing, he added, "We take good care of our sheep."

"Of course we do, but these are some sheep we bought at the last auction. They may have been infected before they came to us and just didn't show the symptoms until now."

Bailey kicked Alex. Alex jumped at the sharp jab and shot Bailey a dirty look. Bailey opened her eyes as wide as possible as if to give her friend a clue that she had an idea. Alex nodded. They'd talk later.

"We've had sheep with hoof rot before," Aunt Darcy said.

"Will they get better?" Bailey's voice came out high, registering her concern and her tender heart.

"Oh yes," Uncle Nathan assured her. "We'll soak their feet in Epsom salts and put medicine on them. And keep their bedding extra clean and dry until they are ready to join the rest of the flock again."

"So where are the lambs now?" Brian asked. "We didn't see any in the barn."

"They're isolated in the old henhouse." Uncle Nathan spooned a mountain of casserole on his plate and dusted it with pepper.

Bailey looked at Brian and Alex. All three raised their eyebrows and exchanged smiles.

●—●—●

In their room that night, Alex checked her e-mail while Bailey got ready for bed. "Here's something from Sydney. I'll read it out loud."

Hi, Bailey and Alex! I found out Gonzo's grandpa, Pedro, disowned Gonzo's dad, Jaime, when he was a rebellious teenager. However, when Pedro learned he had a grandson, he started a relationship with him against Jaime's wishes, continuing their bad relationship. Pedro eventually cut his son completely out of his will and put Gonzo in instead.

Alex looked wide-eyed at Bailey. "Sounds like that could be the motive in our mystery."

"Yes!" Bailey then shared the idea that prompted the kick under the table. "Remember those sheep we saw at Hazelwood Farms?"

"Yeah, they smelled worse than Uncle Nathan's sheep!"

"But remember how sick they seemed? Some could barely walk!"

"Yeah, I remember." Alex looked blankly at Bailey.

"I bet they had hoof rot, and the sheep with the messages came from that flock."

Alex's eyes lit up like twin candles. "You're a genius!" She grabbed Bailey's hands, and they danced around the room in their pajamas. They finally collapsed on the floor in laughter.

"But wait a minute," Alex said breathlessly. "The message said Gonzo was being held captive at Brindle Branch."

"Yeah. . ."

"But we met Gonzo at Hazelwood. It's the wrong farm, and he didn't seem like he was being held against his will anyway."

Bailey's eyebrows came together. "Hmm. You're right." She paused. "I don't have an answer to that right now, and I'm too tired to think it through." Bailey yawned and stretched. "How 'bout if we sleep on it, and maybe something will come to us tomorrow."

"Okay." Alex flipped off the light. "We also need to take a walk down the creek to see if we can learn any more about Brindle Branch Farm."

"And I need to spend extra time shearing to get my time down. It'll be my last day to practice before the big competition. Looks like we have a busy day ahead of us." Bailey yawned again. She heard Alex breathe heavy, no doubt counting sheep.

●—●—●

Friday morning dawned bright and warmer. After a quick breakfast, Bailey and Alex hurried to the barn to start shearing. Alex timed Bailey partway through their morning's work and found she had trimmed off another minute.

"Still not enough to win tomorrow's contest." Bailey's forehead wrinkled.

"Just keep at it. We'll time you again at the end of the morning." Alex smiled and gave Bailey an encouraging pat on the back. "I just *know* you can do this."

Before long, Bailey was guiding her last sheep to the shearing station. She waved Alex down. "Will you time me once more? I'm on my last sheep."

"Sure." Alex set her shears down and came to Bailey's station. "Let me know when you're ready." Alex's finger was poised to push the stopwatch button at Bailey's word. "Remember—just pretend you're uncovering another message on the sheep."

"All right. Ready!" Bailey said.

Alex started the stopwatch, and the shearing began. Fleece fell to the clean barn floor in thick, curly bunches.

Minutes later, Bailey called, "Done!"

Alex punched the button on the stopwatch and checked the time. "Thirteen minutes, thirty-nine seconds. Bailey, you dropped almost two minutes today!"

"Yeah, but it still isn't enough to beat last year's record of twelve minutes, twenty seconds. I'm out of days to practice."

"I still think you have a chance to win. Every time you shear you get faster. When you compete, I bet you'll have your fastest time ever."

"I hope so." Bailey looked to Alex's workstation. "Are you finished with your lambs?"

"I only have two more; then I'm done."

"I'll take one and you do the other. Then we'll be through," Bailey offered. "That will give me a little more practice, and we can get to our detective work sooner."

"Sounds good to me."

After the last lambs were sheared, Bailey asked, "What should we do first?"

"Let's peek at the lambs in the henhouse."

"I'm glad we still have a chance to check their ear tags." Bailey started toward the building the hens had once occupied.

"Me, too!"

Bailey and Alex ran toward the henhouse. They heard the lambs bleating. Bailey pulled the weathered door open and stepped into the shadowy building. Sun poured through glassless windows and spaces between the old wooden wall slats, striping the henhouse in light. A rotten stink permeated the air.

The lambs weren't penned up. They roamed freely in the building, though there wasn't much room. Most limped, their hooves infected.

"Here you are!" Bailey said as she moved closer to the lambs. Then she stopped short. "Alex!"

Alex was just entering through the door.

"It's not them!"

"What?"

"These aren't the lambs with the messages!"

Alex joined Bailey, and the two looked closely at each

sheep. No messages adorned any of them.

"Where could they be?" Alex bit the cuticle on her thumb.

"We need Brian to show us where that other pasture is he told us about yesterday."

"What if they're not there either?"

"Then we need to tell Uncle Nathan that someone stole his sheep." Bailey looked at her watch. "Brian won't be done shearing for another couple of hours. In the meantime, maybe we should take that walk down the creek to see if we can learn anything about Brindle Branch Farm."

"We promised Uncle Nathan we'd stay on this side of the creek."

"There are farms on this side of it, too. We might be able to talk to some of those neighbors." Bailey pulled out her lip balm and smeared on a generous layer.

"Good point," Alex said. "Let's go."

At the first farmhouse they reached, a slender woman wearing blue capris and a floral, button-down sleeveless shirt was weeding a strawberry bed.

"Excuse me," Bailey called.

The woman looked up from her plants. "Yes?"

"I'm Bailey Chang, and this is my friend Alexis. We're visiting my Uncle Nathan who lives just across the pasture."

"Oh yes," the woman replied. "We know Nathan. It's a pleasure to meet you, Bailey." She extended a hand to each of the girls, one at a time. "And you, too, Alexis. I'm Trudy Myers."

"We're doing a bit of research about the area and

wondered if you could help us fill in some gaps." Bailey pulled out her notepad.

"I'd be glad to help if I can," Ms. Myers said.

"We found out the name of this creek used to be Brindle Creek," Alex informed her. "But we found an old sign at the flea market that said BRINDLE BRANCH FARM, and now we're curious about that."

"Brindle Branch Farm?" Ms. Myers pulled another weed. "Yes, I've heard of that."

"You have?" Bailey felt like hugging the woman.

"I haven't lived here so many years that I can say I *remember* it, but I do recall hearing people talk of it."

"What did they say?" Alex asked.

"Not much, just that the men who lived there weren't nice. Didn't take care of their farm, I guess."

"Anything else?" Bailey asked.

"No, not that I can think of."

"About those men," Alex questioned. "Do you know their names or how many of them there were?"

"Heavens! I haven't the foggiest notion of their names, but I think I heard there were two men." Ms. Myers eyed Bailey and Alex and smiled. "What are you girls up to anyway?"

"Just research, that's all," Bailey answered. "Do you know where their farm was?"

"Sorry, no," Ms. Myers said.

"Thanks for your help," Alex said.

"Yeah, we've learned a lot already!" Bailey flipped her notepad closed.

"Anytime," Ms. Myers answered, bending over to pull another handful of weeds. "Good luck!"

Bailey and Alex went on to the next farm, where an elderly man was scattering grain for his chickens.

"Hello!" Bailey greeted him with a smile and wave.

The man looked up from his chores. "Hello yourself!" His wrinkled face crinkled in a crooked grin. Gray hair poked out on all sides beneath his straw hat. "What can I do ya for?"

Above the clucking of the chickens, Bailey introduced herself and Alex. Then she told him they were doing research of the area.

"Research, huh? Sounds important! Oh, by the way, the name's Don."

The girls shook his leathery hand.

"Now let's hear more about this research you're doin'."

"We're trying to learn about a place called Brindle Branch Farm. We found a sign at the flea market with that name carved in it." Alex kept a close eye on the speckled hens pecking and scratching the ground around her. A huge red rooster eyed them from a distance.

Don rubbed his gray, whiskery chin. "Brindle Branch Farm. . .yes, I remember that. Its name changed a few years back."

"It did?" Bailey's neck jutted forward, and her eyes popped.

"Yes, ma'am. Changed ownership about the same time, too." Don tossed another handful of grain from the cloth bag hanging over his shoulder, and the chickens ran to peck it up, clucking away.

"What did the name change to?" Alex asked.

"One of those new flavors of coffee creamers, as I remember."

"Huh?" Bailey wondered if the man was a taco short of a combo plate.

"You know—Irish cream, French vanilla, hazelnut, something like that."

"Hazelwood maybe?" Alex asked, her eyes gleaming.

"Hazelwood! That's it!" Don clapped his hand against his lean thigh. "It's just over there on the other side of the creek." He pointed a crooked finger in the direction of Yeller, Dude, and Rude's house.

"Did you ever meet the owners?" Bailey asked.

"Knew the first owners." Don's eyes dulled and his voice grew husky. "Good people."

"I'm sorry," Alex said softly.

"How about the new owners?" Bailey gently pushed. "Do you know them, too?"

"Tried to, but they keep to themselves. They let the place go to pot."

Alex twirled a curl around her finger. "We heard that only men live there. No wife or children."

"True enough," Don agreed. "Just three men who don't care two hoots about taking care of their property or their animals."

"Three men?" Bailey asked. "You sure about that?"

"Sure as my name's Don Jeffers! There are three men, but two of them do most of the work, what little work they do. The other one stays pretty much out of sight. The two told me once that their brother isn't right in the head. They said I shouldn't pay any attention if he hollers or waves his arms around. Said he's kind of crazy."

Bailey nodded. "We can't thank you enough for the information. You've been a great help to our research."

"My pleasure," Don said. "You come on back anytime."

Bailey and Alex walked back toward the creek. "Incredible!" Bailey said as soon as they were out of Don's earshot.

"No kidding!" Alex turned a cartwheel on the soft, cool grass. "Hazelwood and Brindle Branch are the same place!"

"That's weird what he said about the third guy. Do you really think he's their brother? Or that he has all those problems they say he has?"

"Who knows?" Alex pushed her curly hair behind her ears. "Guess it could be a family business, but they don't seem very friendly like brothers should."

Bailey checked the time. "It's still a little early, but Brian may be almost done with his shearing. Let's start back home."

The girls turned back the way they'd come, chatting as they walked. Soon they were across the creek from the pasture of sick sheep they'd seen yesterday.

"There are those poor sheep again." Alex plugged her nose.

"Wait a minute!" Bailey stopped and squinted her eyes as she stared at them.

"What?"

"I think some of those sheep have writing on them!"

The Mystery at Hazelwood

"See? Look at that little one in the corner." Bailey leaned in and pointed so Alex's eye could follow her finger.

"Yeah! I'm sure those are our sheep!"

Bailey chewed her lower lip. "What should we do?"

"Tell Uncle Nathan someone's stolen some of his lambs."

Bailey stood silent for a moment. Finally, she nodded. "I guess we'll have to. I don't know what else to do."

Both girls were surprised when Bailey's phone rang.

"Hello? Oh hi, Kate. . . . You did?"

Alex put her ear close to the phone.

"Hang on, Kate. I'm going to put you on speaker." Bailey pressed the button. "Okay, go."

"I found out how someone could be held captive so long," Kate repeated. "Especially if he's allowed outside, as apparently Yeller is."

"Great!" Alex said. "What's the secret?"

"They could have Yeller hooked up with a house arrest bracelet that tells them if he leaves the property."

"How's it work?" Bailey asked.

"It's equipped with a GPS system that shows the

person's location on a monitor."

"Impressive," Alex said.

"But wouldn't they have known if Yeller was off the property?" Bailey asked.

"They should have seen it on the monitor," Kate confirmed. "And an alarm is supposed to sound when a breach occurs."

"Something doesn't add up." Alex picked a hangnail from her finger. "Anything else we should know?"

"That's about it."

"Good work, Kate." Bailey wished she could hug her friend. "Thanks."

"No problem-o," Kate said.

"Give Biscuit a scratch behind the ears for me," Alex said.

Kate squealed. "Biscuit! Get down! I think he heard that. He's trying to lick the phone!"

The girls laughed and updated her on the stolen lambs. "Unbelievable!"

"We're on our way home to tell Uncle Nathan now." Bailey's shoulders slumped.

"Good luck," Kate said. "I'll be praying for you!"

At home, Uncle Nathan strolled from the barn toward the house.

"Uncle Nathan!" Bailey called.

Her uncle stopped and turned. "What's up?"

"We need to talk to you about some of your lambs."

"I'm all ears," he said.

"We think some have been stolen." Bailey watched her uncle closely.

He screwed up his face. "Stolen? Why do you think that?"

"Because some of the lambs we sheared had messages written on them, and now they're gone!" Alex spilled.

"At first we thought they were the ones you separated because of hoof rot, but they weren't," Bailey explained.

"And we saw some marked sheep at the ranch across the creek that looked just like the ones we sheared," Alex added.

"We didn't go over there!" Bailey assured him. "We saw them from *our* side of the creek."

Uncle Nathan held up his hand. "Whoa!" he said. "Back up. Messages on sheep?"

"Yeah," Bailey answered.

"What kind of messages?"

"They said, 'Help Gonzo held captive Brindle Branch.'" Bailey grinned. It felt good to finally tell an adult what they'd uncovered.

"Anyone else know about this?" Uncle Nathan asked.

"Only Brian," Bailey answered.

"And the Camp Club Girls," Alex added.

Uncle Nathan's eyebrows raised in question.

"They're our friends from camp who help us solve mysteries," Bailey said.

"And you have a mystery to solve?" Uncle Nathan prodded.

"We think so." Bailey shrugged. "Why else would there

be messages on sheep?"

"Good point." Uncle Nathan exhaled. "So you think the neighbors stole the sheep with the messages."

"Right." Bailey nodded.

Uncle Nathan looked toward the neighbor's ranch. "Can you show me?"

"Sure!" Alex's eyes sparkled. "You'll need binoculars if you want a good look."

Uncle Nathan went inside, returning with a pair of binoculars around his neck. "All set. Lead the way."

Bailey and Alex took off toward the dilapidated house. When they got to the creek, they walked along its bank a short distance and then pointed to the pasture on the other side.

"See?" Bailey said. "They're over there behind the fence."

Uncle Nathan looked through the binoculars.

"Do you see some young sheep with strange black markings?" Bailey asked.

"Sure do," he answered. "My binoculars aren't strong enough to read the ear tag though."

"May I look?" Bailey reached out her hand.

Uncle Nathan took the binoculars from around his neck and handed them to her.

Bailey scanned the pasture, looking for the marked sheep. "There's one!" she announced.

"Which one is it?" Alex asked.

"Brindle Branch."

Alex nodded. "Yep. Those are your sheep, Uncle Nathan."

"How many had messages?" he asked.

"Three. I bet they stole all three so no one would see their messages." Bailey kicked a rock into the creek.

"All right, girls." Uncle Nathan hung the binoculars back around his neck. "Let's go call the sheriff."

Twenty minutes later, two deputies came to the house. "I'm Officer Cahill," said the dark-haired one, "and this is my partner, Officer Hamilton."

"Come in," Uncle Nathan said. He introduced Bailey and Alex. "They're the ones who brought this to my attention. They spotted the sheep from across the creek. Here, have a seat." Uncle Nathan waved his hand toward the living room. The officers settled into the easy chairs across from the couch where Bailey and Alex sat. Uncle Nathan grabbed a kitchen chair for himself.

"Tell us what you saw." Officer Cahill spoke gently to the girls and listened attentively.

"Wait a minute," he interrupted their story. "You say these sheep had messages written on them?"

"Yes, sir." Bailey nodded solemnly.

"What did they say?"

Alex told him and explained how the message was spread between three sheep.

"Interesting." Officer Cahill rubbed his chin.

Bailey looked at Alex with questioning eyes and received a nod of approval.

"Sir, there's more."

"More?" the officer asked.

"We think we may have figured out the Marshall Gonzalez case."

"What?" Uncle Nathan jumped up as if he'd sat on a tack. "I'm sorry, officers. I don't know anything about this."

"Tell me what you know." Officer Hamilton knelt so he was eye-to-eye with Bailey sitting on the couch.

Bailey licked her lips and looked around nervously.

"It's all right. Don't be afraid."

Bailey and Alex told them everything—from the marked sheep, to the nighttime visit from Yeller, to discovering the original names of the ranch and creek.

Officer Cahill took notes furiously as the girls spoke. When they finally slowed down, so did his pen. He looked at his partner with a grin and a nod.

"I am very impressed with your detective work, girls," Officer Hamilton said. "We'll check this out and get back to you."

"Will you go to Hazelwood Ranch?" Bailey asked.

"Yes, we'll pay them a visit. Hopefully, they'll cooperate and you'll have your sheep back within a few hours. But it may take us longer to piece together all you've told us about the Marshall Gonzalez case."

"Don't take too long getting back to us!" Bailey blurted. "We have to leave tomorrow evening!"

Officer Cahill laughed. "We'll try to work fast!"

●—●—●

After dinner the policemen were back at their door.

"Mr. Chang?" Officer Cahill held a clipboard. "We have

some sheep to deliver."

Uncle Nathan clapped his hands. "Hot dog!" he said. "So they *were* my sheep!"

"They were indeed. The ear tags showed your ID on them, so there wasn't much the thieves could say."

"Did you haul them off to jail?" Brian appeared over his dad's shoulder, excitement blazing in his eyes.

"They're being booked."

"What about the Gonzalez case?" Bailey asked.

"We're still working on that." Officer Cahill smiled at Bailey. "But we're pretty sure you're on to something."

Bailey and Alex grinned. Their hard work was paying off.

"I'll help you unload those sheep." Uncle Nathan followed the officer to a livestock trailer. The sun was setting, and the men worked quickly to get the lambs back into the pasture with their mothers. The ewes nuzzled their babies, and the lambs baaed their dismay at having been away.

●—●—●

"Alex, wake up! It's Saturday!"

Alex rolled over and rubbed her sleepy eyes. "Huh?"

"Wake up! Today's the sheep-shearing competition. And we'll find out about our investigation!"

Alex's feet hit the floor running. She jumped into her clothes and shoes. "I'm ready. Let's go!"

The aroma of bacon and eggs greeted the girls as they charged down the stairs.

"Good morning, sleepyheads!" Aunt Darcy called over her shoulder as she flipped the eggs.

"Mornin', Aunt Darcy!"

Uncle Nathan entered from outside. "Well, look who's up!" He planted a kiss on top of Bailey's head and ruffled Alex's hair. "Sleep good?"

Bailey and Alex both nodded.

"The police already called this morning," Aunt Darcy said. "They're on their way over."

"Now?" Bailey asked. "What'd they say?"

"Just that they'd talk to us when they get here." Aunt Darcy set a plate full of bacon on the table and slid a fried egg onto each plate. "So I suggest we eat fast."

Uncle Nathan blessed the food then passed the bacon to Alex. Aunt Darcy poured milk while Bailey and Alex ate their eggs. They'd started clearing the table when someone knocked. Uncle Nathan went to answer it.

"Good morning, Officer Cahill, Officer Hamilton." Uncle Nathan waved them inside. A third, shorter man appeared from behind the two policemen.

"Mr. Chang, it gives me great pleasure to introduce to you Marshall Gonzalez."

"Wha–. . .*the* Marshall Gonzalez?" Uncle Nathan stammered.

"Marshall Gonzalez?" Bailey pushed past Uncle Nathan, with Alex behind her. A cleaned-up Yeller stood before them, grinning from ear to ear. "Yeller!"

"Yeller?" Officer Cahill looked from Gonzo to Bailey.

"That's just the nickname Bailey gave him 'cause he yelled to us the first time we saw him," Alex explained.

"Come in, come in," Aunt Darcy said, her manners edging out her astonishment. She bustled past her husband and pulled the men inside. "Have a seat. I'll make some fresh coffee."

"But that other guy told us *he* was Gonzo!" Bailey cried.

"He confessed to that lie," Officer Hamilton said. "Said he was trying to confuse you about Marshall's identity in case you were nosing around and knew anything."

Alex laughed. "He doesn't know us very well, does he, Bailey?"

"We'd never quit that easily!" Bailey giggled. "So if you're the real Gonzo, the other two men must have been your captors, as we suspected."

Gonzo nodded. "They were hired by my own father who wanted my money. They kidnapped me and made me wear that house arrest bracelet for seven years! That's why I don't look much like that newspaper photo. I'm thinner and older now."

"Why did you only try to contact the girls?" Suspicion tinged Uncle Nathan's voice. "Why didn't you try to tell an adult?"

"My kidnappers told everyone I was their crazy brother and not to pay any attention to what I said or did." Marshall's head drooped. "When I saw these girls, I thought maybe they'd believe me since they were new around here and probably hadn't heard about the crazy brother."

Uncle Nathan nodded. "I do remember hearing the

151

gossip about you, now that I think back. Guess I just took it for truth."

Bailey cocked her head. "But if you wore a house arrest bracelet, how did you sneak out that night you came over here?"

"My captors drank so much alcohol they passed out." Marshall looked at Bailey, his eyes serious. "That's when I came over here. I'm sorry if I scared you. I was desperate for someone to know I wasn't dead!"

"But when they woke up, didn't their monitor show you'd been gone?" Alex's eyebrows furrowed.

"Yep. They woke up while I was gone and came looking for me. I heard them yell at me while I was up in your tree. When I turned to look, I lost my balance and fell."

Brian stumbled into the kitchen bleary-eyed. He looked more confused than ever as he saw the strangers. The girls brought him up to speed on what was going on.

"So you wrote those messages on the sheep with a paint stick?" Brian asked.

"I did," Gonzo replied rather proudly.

"So what's next for you, Marshall?" Uncle Nathan asked.

"Well, thanks to these gals, my relatives will not get my fortune!" He looked with gratitude at Bailey and Alex. "I feel the whole world has opened up to me. I used to be an unhappy, lonely man. But after what I've been through, I'd like a chance to start over right here in Peoria. I hope to fix up my ranch and be the good shepherd my sheep deserve."

"Looks like *the* Good Shepherd watched out for you in

spite of all your troubles," Bailey said softly.

"Indeed He has," Marshall replied. "I hope to get to know Him better in the future."

"We'd better let these good people get on with their day." Officer Cahill stood to leave. "We knew the girls would be anxious to find out how their super sleuthing turned out. You did a great job figuring out this mystery, girls. We owe you a hearty thanks."

"You don't need to thank us. We love sleuthing!" Alex beamed at the officer.

"We're just glad Mr. Gonzalez is safe again. Thanks for coming by so we could meet you." Bailey stuck out her hand for him to shake.

Gonzo took her hand and pulled her into a big hug. Tears welled in his eyes. "I can never thank you enough!"

While Uncle Nathan walked the officers and Gonzo to their car, Aunt Darcy picked up empty coffee cups and set them in the sink. She leaned against the counter, eyeing Bailey and Alex with a smile. "It's amazing what you girls accomplished in only six days."

When Uncle Nathan returned, he noticed the time. "Are you ready to go to the big shearing competition?"

"I almost forgot!" Bailey replied. "But I'm ready."

"Then let's load up!" her uncle said.

As they pulled up to the fairgrounds, the smells of popcorn and hot dogs filled the air. The hum of people, mingled with the baaing of sheep, made a chaotic, festive atmosphere.

They sat in the stands watching kids in Bailey's age group compete. The first, a nine-year-old girl like Bailey, worked slowly, with an ending time of twenty-two minutes, thirteen seconds. Then a ten-year-old boy gave it his best shot, finishing at twelve minutes, forty-three seconds.

Bailey felt a hand on her elbow. "Come on, it's almost your turn." Uncle Nathan helped her stand. Her legs suddenly felt like jelly. *What if I can't handle the sheep? Maybe I'll embarrass myself and Uncle Nathan, too.*

Alex grabbed Bailey's hand. "I'll be here cheering and praying for you like mad. Your last practice time of twelve minutes, twenty seconds beats everyone we've seen so far!"

Bailey gave a weak smile. How would she ever be a famous actress if she let her nerves get to her like this? Inhaling deeply, she let out her breath slowly. "With God's help I'm going to beat all those times!"

"That's the spirit!" Aunt Darcy hugged Bailey. "Remember, we're proud of you no matter what!"

Bailey nodded and followed Uncle Nathan to the competitors' waiting area. By the time they reached it, only one girl was ahead of her. She had the fastest time yet at twelve minutes, five seconds.

"That's fifteen seconds faster than last year's winning time!" Bailey wailed.

Uncle Nathan squatted, took Bailey by the shoulders, and looked directly into her black-brown eyes. "Don't you worry about anybody's time but your own, you hear? Just do your best."

Bailey nodded and swallowed a lump in her throat. Her mouth turned to cotton. She put on another coat of lip balm.

"Bailey Chang!" the announcer called.

Uncle Nathan nudged Bailey toward the arena. Bailey had never felt so small. The crowd cheered, and a woolly sheep was brought to her. A timekeeper stood close by.

Bailey whispered a quick prayer then flipped on the shears. The timekeeper started the stopwatch. Bailey ran the shears up and down the lamb's body, and fleece fell like a soft blanket. She imagined a message appearing beneath the fallen wool and pretended Gonzo's life depended on her uncovering it quickly. Minutes later, she switched off the shears, and the timekeeper punched the stopwatch.

"Eleven minutes, seventeen seconds!" Raising Bailey's hand in the air, he announced, "A new record!"

Uncle Nathan ran to Bailey and scooped her into his arms. "Way to go, Bailey! You were awesome!"

"I didn't win yet, Uncle Nathan," Bailey cautioned. "There's still one more contestant."

"I know." Uncle Nathan let her slide back to the ground. "But I'm so proud of you."

Aunt Darcy raced toward them. "Bailey! I can't believe how fast you were!" She wrapped her in a bear hug and kissed her cheek.

"You were amazing!" Alex said.

"Hey, kid!" Brian sauntered up, cool as ever. "You were almost as good as me!"

"*If* you'd had the nerve to enter the competition!" Bailey teased.

"I didn't want to compete against you! Maybe I'll give it a try next year." Brian messed up Bailey's hair.

The group turned their attention to the last competitor as the announcer's voice echoed through the loudspeaker. "Last year's champion in the nine- to twelve-year-old group, Jackson Pruitt!"

The arena exploded with applause, and the crowd rose to their feet.

The announcer continued. "Jackson set a new record at twelve minutes, twenty seconds last year. Bailey Chang already broke that record today! Will Jackson be able to beat her time and keep his title?"

Jackson and his sheep took their places. The race was on! His arm flew, the shears buzzed, the fleece fell as silently as the crowd had become. Moments later, he turned off the shears.

"Eleven minutes, forty seconds! Bailey Chang is our new champion with her time of eleven minutes, seventeen seconds! Bailey Chang, come on out here!"

Uncle Nathan, Aunt Darcy, Brian, and Alex all walked into the arena with Bailey. The judge draped a "Shearing Master" sash across her shoulder and presented her with a huge trophy. Thunderous applause shook the stands.

Bailey looked around her. All this was for her? She quietly bowed her head. *Thank You, God. You did this for me.* When she raised her head, tears filled her eyes as

Marshall Gonzalez came from the crowd and placed an enormous bouquet of yellow roses in her arms.

Gonzo was free and safe, she'd won the shearing competition, and she'd enjoyed a whole week with Alex. This spring break was more than she'd dreamed it would be!

If you enjoyed
BAILEY'S PEORIA PROBLEM
be sure to read other
CAMP CLUB GIRLS
books from BARBOUR PUBLISHING

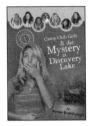

Book 1: Mystery at Discovery Lake

ISBN 978-1-60260-267-0

Book 2: Sydney's DC Discovery

ISBN 978-1-60260-268-7

Book 3: McKenzie's Montana Mystery

ISBN 978-1-60260-269-4

Book 4: Alexis and the Sacramento Surprise

ISBN 978-1-60260-270-0

Book 5: Kate's Philadelphia Frenzy

ISBN 978-1-60260-271-7

AVAILABLE WHEREVER BOOKS ARE SOLD.